OVER MY DEAD BODY

an Al Pennyback mystery

CHARLES RAY

North Potomac, MD

This book is a work of fiction. Names, descriptions, places, and incidents are products of the author's imagination, or are used fictionally. Any resemblance to actual events or persons, living or dead, is purely coincidental.

The reproduction or distribution, by any means, including electronic distribution, is expressly prohibited without the written consent of the copyright holder, except for fair use quotes in connection with reviews.

For information about this and other works of this author, contact the author at charlesray.author@gmail.com.

Independent authors survive through word of mouth referrals. If you enjoyed this book, please consider leaving a brief review on Amazon, or any other site to let other readers know.

Printed in the United States of America.

ISBN: 0692856412
ISBN-13: 978-0692856413

Dedication

It's common on a dedication page to thank everyone who contributed in any way to the creation of a book. For this, and my other works, such a list would be far too long, for I've been inspired and helped along the way by so many people. So, I'll just say thanks to everyone who believed in me, when there were times I wasn't sure that I believed in myself, to everyone who held out a hand when I needed to be pulled out of the doldrums. You know who you are, for you're the type person who does this for everyone. I would also like to dedicate this book to those few readers who keep coming back to read my feeble attempts at storytelling, who give me comments from time to time on what works, and, more importantly, what doesn't. You are why I do this. You, the reader, are why any writer sits down day after day, pounding out word after word, page after page. I hope you will find something to like about this book, and if you do, that you'll take the time to write a review—no matter how short—because, reviews draw attention to books, attract new readers, and that's what we writers are all about, getting more people to read what we write.

Charles Ray

Chapter 1

The highway sang beneath my tires. The whine of tires on the pavement was accompanied by Willie Nelson's gravelly voice coming from the radio, singing 'Mama, don't let your babies grow up to be cowboys.' I'd been fiddling with the radio since hitting the road, and a country station was the only clear, non-talk station I could find. Fortunately, I grew up listening to a station that broadcast out of Del Rio, Texas in the fifties and sixties, playing a mix of country, blues, and rock and roll, and listening to Gene Autry, the Singing Cowboy, on our black and white television, so I'm not totally turned off by most country music. Added to that, Nelson's plaintive sound is not all that far from the blues, which is country music's black cousin, or, given that blues was probably created first, country music is blues' black cousin.

I, however, did not feel like singing. What I felt like was doing a U-turn, going back to the George Bush Intercontinental Airport on the north side of Houston, and catching the first flight back to Washington. Sure, I was more than halfway to my destination, but it was only a two-hour drive back to Houston down U.S. 59; and significantly less than that to the airport.

My memories of this highway were mixed. I vaguely recalled being piled in the back of our old Ford station wagon for the five hour drive from our little town in Shelby County, hard by the Louisiana state line and more Cajun than Texas, to Houston, which was, in the 1960s the biggest city in Texas, but not yet the fourth largest city in the United States, and except for Third Ward which was the predominantly black section of the city, not all that hospitable or welcoming to people of color, but was nonetheless friendlier than Shelby County or any town in Louisiana. Back then, the high buildings, constant traffic and concrete sidewalks were a novelty to a kid accustomed to one- and two-story buildings and dirt roads, and my mom liked to shop at the big stores like Dillards, even though, just as they did in Shelby County, she had to wait for white customers to be served first.

"If I have to wait, I should at least be able to buy first-class merchandise," she always said. And, that was true. The little clothing store in our town sold dresses that looked like they'd gone out of style when Woodrow Wilson was president.

In 2003, Houston had changed. Now, officially the fourth largest city in the country, after gobbling up many of the small towns encircling it, and with two beltways, the outer one large enough to include Washington, DC *and* Baltimore, people of color could live anywhere in the city they pleased, and no longer had to wait to be served in department stores. Unlike the rest of Texas, which was controlled by Republicans, Houston was a stronghold of Democrats, and now they weren't the ones wearing white sheets and burning crosses like they'd been when I was a kid.

In other words, it was almost a nice place to visit. Unless it's where you came from, or near where you came from. Then, as a cousin of mine whose name I can never remember always said, "The best view of Houston, or anywhere else in Texas, for that matter, is the one in your rearview mirror as you're leaving." According to him, there were only two kinds of Texans, regardless of their color; the ones who never left, and the ones who never came back.

When I graduated from high school and, against my mother's wishes, joined the army instead of going off to Prairie View College on the valedictorian scholarship I'd been offered, I vowed to be in the second category. When my parents were swept away in a hurricane that hit the coast south of Galveston while they were visiting a relative who had a house on the 'colored' section of the beach, I'd broken that vow to attend the memorial service. Their bodies were never recovered, so there were no 'graves' to visit, and when the service was over, I jumped in my rented car and left, again vowing never to return.

I'd broken that vow a second time a few years back when a distant relative left me some property just north of Houston, and I'd had to personally present myself to the court to settle the estate. During that visit, I'd gotten caught up in a murder case that, fortunately, turned out okay, got the property settled, and when I settled back in my seat on the plane flying me back to DC, thought I was finally done with the place.

It was not to be. Family came first; even distant relatives that you could barely remember had a call on you. When they asked for help, you helped. Wherever you were, unless it was in the middle of a war zone in the middle of a battle, you dropped what you were doing and came to their aid. That's just the way I was raised.

Winston Jones, first or second cousin on my mother's side of the family, I could never figure it out, had to be in his late seventies by my reckoning. He lived in the little town of Poseyville, near the intersection of US Highways 59 and 69, southwest of the town of Diboll. Diboll is a town of less than 6,000, and is in Angelina County, while Poseyville has about 1,200 inhabitants and is in Coquilla County. So, while the county government authorities responsible for things in Poseyville are in the Coquilla county seat, Jacksonville, they're closer to Diboll, so except for the sheriff, who has no jurisdiction outside the county where voters have elected him, they get most everything from Diboll. If that sounds confusing, it is, but then, almost everything about Texas outside the big cities is confusing unless you live there, and then, that's just the way it is. In Winston's case, though, it was this geographic and jurisdictional conundrum that motivated him to look my phone number up and call me.

* * *

When Heather, my partner, who also handles incoming phone calls—a holdover from

4

being originally hired as my secretary and administrative assistant, and the fact that she's a hell of a lot better on the phone than me—informed me that my Cousin Winston Jones from Texas was on the line, my response was all too predictable.

"Hang up on him," I said. "I don't know anyone named Winston Jones."

In my defense, the name, when she said, rang no bells at all, but then, in rural Texas, just about everyone is everyone else's cousin. At the memorial service for my parents nearly 300 people came and half of them introduced themselves to me as a cousin.

"Come on Al," she said. "That would be rude. Besides, he said you probably wouldn't remember him."

"Well, he got that part right. What does he want?"

"He wants to speak to you. He says it's family business."

"Ask him to prove he's my cousin."

She made a snorting sound over the intercom. "How am I supposed to do that?"

"Hey," I said. "You're now a hotshot private eye like me, you figure it out."

With an unladylike growl, she broke the connection. A few seconds later, the machine made a warbling sound. I answered.

"Okay, smart ass," she said. "He said your mother had a friend named Aletha, and the two of them used to play dress up like English princesses."

That brought me up short. I remembered my mother telling that story when I was little, and my father ribbing her about two little black girls in rural East Texas pretending to be white English royalty. It had been a story told only inside the family, so whoever was on the phone, if not related, had been close enough to have heard it.

"Put him through," I said.

There was a crackle, a kind of 'zzt!' sound, and a click, and then a gravelly voice, "Hello, anybody there . . . hello."

"Al Pennyback here," I said. "To whom am I speaking?"

"Oh, hey, I ain't been cut off," the voice said. "This here's Winston Jones, Cousin Winston, is you little Al?"

"There is nothing little about me, sir, and I'm afraid I don't recall having a cousin by the name of Winston Jones."

A long pause left me expecting to hear a dial tone indicating he'd hung up, but then his voice came back on the line.

"Aw, I see. Last time I saw you, I reckon you was 'bout ten or so. You pro'bly remember me as Cousin Wide Body."

Then it all came rushing back into my mind. Wide Body. The cousin everyone snickered at behind their hands because he was so big. To ten-year-old me, he was like a man mountain. His shoulders were so wide he had to turn sideways to enter our living room. He had arms and legs like tree trunks, and hands so big one of them could engulf your entire head. I remember my mother stage whispering to my father that Wide Body . . . Winston . . . weighed at least 300 pounds, and at that time he was somewhere in his mid-twenties.

"Ah, yes, Cousin Wide, er Cousin Winston, I remember you. My partner said you wanted to discuss family business; what's the business?"

His response was vague; something about an oil company and a neighbor trying to evict him from his property, a modest-sized farm outside the town of Poseyville, and him getting no help from local authorities. He'd read in some magazine, or seen something on TV—I didn't get that part clearly—about this detective, Al Pennyback, in Washington, DC, who helped people in need, and he'd wondered if that was his little cousin, so he'd had his daughter track down my phone number and called me. I'm not great on getting things out of people over the phone, which is why I usually let Heather deal with that aspect of our business, so when Cousin Winston asked if I could come to Texas and help him out of a pickle, I thought about it for all of thirty seconds before agreeing.

* * *

Now, as I got farther and farther away from Houston, into an area where low, wood-frame houses sat hunkered down among trash-littered yards beside the road, I was beginning to question the wisdom of my decision. A nasally voiced singer replaced Willie Nelson, singing some song about his girl leaving him alone at a dance. I much preferred Willie's song advising mamas not to let their babies pick guitars and drive old trucks, advice that most women in East Texas seem to have ignored, because there were two old pickups to every other kind of car on U.S. 59, almost all of them with gun racks and being driven by crusty looking characters of various ages wearing battered Stetsons. The main livelihoods of the people of East Texas, at least when I was a kid growing up there, was farming, cotton, sugar cane, and melons; the lumber industry, mostly converting the local evergreens to pulp for the paper industry; and livestock, mainly chickens and dairy cows. That didn't stop every man, woman, and child, black, white, or Mexican, in the area of thinking of themselves as cowboys, and dressing the part, or at least what they thought cowboys dressed like.

In his book, *You Can't Go Home Again*, Thomas Wolfe wrote, 'Some things will never change. Some things will always be the same.' Driving through countryside that in 2003 looked depressingly the way it had looked in the 1960s as I peered at it through the grimy window of a Greyhound bus taking me out of the state to start army basic training, I felt that Wolfe, who was born in North Carolina, but spent most of his time in the northeast, mainly Boston and New York City, had been writing about East Texas. After more than 40 years, I had the feeling that I could find my way around without a map or asking directions, because nothing seemed to have changed.

Doubts were beginning to creep in.

But, I wouldn't turn around. Family was in trouble, and Al Pennyback never leaves family or friend in the lurch.

Chapter 2

I passed through Diboll at around 3:00 pm. There wasn't much to see of the town that straddles US 59, and no reason to stop. What I did see of it didn't look worth bothering with anyway. Thirty minutes later, I entered the outskirts of Lufkin. The county seat of Angelina County, with a population of around 35,000, it's a cross between a small cow town and a tiny city. A bit more prosperous looking than the other small towns I'd driven through. I didn't remember it from the road trips when I was a kid, but had read about it in the news earlier in February when debris from the Space Shuttle Columbia fell in and around it after the vessel exploded shortly after reentering the Earth's atmosphere. Now, four months after the disaster, there wasn't a person outside the town who remembered its name.

U.S. 59 intersected with U.S. 69 near the center of town. I made the right turn onto 69, keeping well within the speed limit as I passed modern buildings owned by the oil well equipment industry towering over frame buildings with false fronts that made them look like sets from a western movie, and then, as if someone had drawn a line in the dirt, exited the town at the southeast and was back in East Texas farm country.

While lumber was big here, and there were a few oil derricks pumping away in some of the fields, there were also big, low poultry sheds, dairy barns, and fields of corn, cotton, melons, and various vegetable crops. I even passed one farm that grew sugar cane.

I was pretty sure that there was a more direct route from Diboll to Poseyville, probably one or two farm to market roads, but had no desire to end up driving around the back country looking for it, and risk getting lost, even if driving to Lufkin and doubling back did add a half hour to my trip.

It was approaching 5:00 when I saw the white metal sign affixed to a rusting metal pole, 'WELCOME TO POSEYVILLE, Pop. 1,160.'

Just past the sign, I pulled onto the shoulder and, with the engine still running, fished Winston's directions from my shirt pocket. He'd given some convoluted directions on how to find his place from the entrance to town, which Heather had translated from my chicken scratch to neatly typed lines of text.

The road leading to Winston's house was the second turn to the left past the city limit sign. According to what he'd told me, it was Shelby Street, but there was no sign at the second street I came to, causing me some doubt, but I turned left and took that unmarked street anyway. In the little town I grew up in, the town council never appropriated a budget for street signs in the 'colored' section of town, using the justification that everyone who lived there knew the streets already, and those who didn't live there didn't need to know. I operated under the assumption that Poseyville was pretty much the same. If the pot-holed condition of the street over which I drove was any indication, I'd made the right assumption.

Thick stands of pine, oak, persimmon, and hickory trees lined both sides of the two-lane blacktop for the first mile, and then gave way to small- to medium-sized fields with lush crops of corn and other crops surrounded by barbed wire fences, or irregular yards with one-story wood frame houses, some prosperous looking and neatly painted, some with tin roofs and unpainted walls bleached by the sun. Prosperous or not, they all had assorted pickups and old-model cars parked in the front yards. A few had small barns or storage buildings behind the main house. Barefooted children, their dark skin glistening with sweat, stopped their play in one front yard as I drove past, their big eyes and swiveling heads tracking me as I passed. In another yard, a bent old lady sat on a porch in a rocking chair. She stopped rocking, and sat forward in the chair, staring hard at me.

I recognized their reactions. There was a stranger—me—in their midst. Phones would be ringing from one end of the road to the other, and people would be talking over back fences and from front porches, trying to figure out just who the hell the guy in the Alamo rental car was. The fact that it was a silver Toyota 4-Runner was scandalous enough here in Ford truck country, but it was brand new and being driven by a black man who wasn't wearing overalls and/or a Stetson would have the rumor mill buzzing at full pitch. I had no doubt that Cousin Winston would know of my arrival long before I arrived at his house.

And, I wasn't wrong.

Winston Jones' farm was hard to miss. For starters, as he'd told me on the phone, his 500 acres was the biggest black-owned farm in Coquilla County, and the third largest in the Poseyville area. And, just in case that wasn't enough information to help you find it, the sign that arched across the big gate at the road up to his house had the words, 'Arcadia Acres, Winston Jones, proprietor' in big black letters. I turned right, passed under the arch, and in a cloud of red dust, made my way to my cousin's front yard.

The house was two floors, and the white walls looked like they'd been recently painted. A screened-in porch ran across the front. The sandy driveway did a loop around a circular bed of roses with a small evergreen tree in the center. Behind the house and to the right was a large metal building that I recognized as a dairy barn, and to the left four long low buildings that I knew to be chicken sheds, looking big enough to contain 10,000 birds in each. Behind these structures and stretching toward the horizon were neatly planted fields, green with whatever crops were growing.

A new looking red Ford F150 double cab pickup sat in the left arc of the loop. I pulled the Toyota in behind it, turned off the engine, and sat there for a few seconds, listening to the ticking sounds from under the hood.

When the ticking stopped, I stepped out and faced the wide door in the screen covering the porch. I could see a large shadow moving behind the screen. The screen door, set in the center of the porch, was higher and wider than your normal door, and when it swung open, I could see why. Winston Jones was as tall and wide as I remembered.

Nearly seven feet tall, with shoulders spanning three feet, a massive chest and a rounded belly that despite its hugeness didn't sag, shirtless and wearing overalls with one shoulder strap hanging down over his massive biceps, my cousin, Winston Jones, looked like a large statue carved from dark wood. His face was a jumble of angles and curves, with prominent cheeks and wide-set brown eyes that seemed to be forever smiling. His head was completely shaved and shone like a brown, bowling ball. Fleshy lips turned up in a smile as he came down the steps to greet me. The steps sagged and groaned in protest as he stepped on them.

A huge, brown, work-hardened hand was thrust in my direction.

"Well, if it ain't my long lost cousin, Little Al," he said in the booming voice I remembered that used to scare the crap out of me as a kid.

Chapter 3

I'm not small. I'm six feet tall and weigh just over two hundred pounds. My years of martial arts training have left my own oversized hands gnarled, but my right hand was lost in Winston's huge mitt.

I hadn't been called 'Little Al' in a long time. Winston was about the only relative I remembered who never saddled me with the name my mother gave me. Alfred Einstein, because of her adoration of the German scientist, combined with my father's family name, Pennyback, made me the target of more ribbing growing up than the school nerds—at least, until I got my growth spurt and learned to fight. After that, except for a few holdouts in my family who insisted on the southern custom of addressing people by their full first and middle names, I was 'Al' to everyone, except Winston, who called me 'Little Al' until I graduated from high school and left to join the army. Of course, back then, at nearly seven feet and over three hundred pounds, everyone else was 'little' to him, and even with my prowess at fisticuffs I wouldn't have lasted ten seconds in a confrontation with him.

"I'm not so little anymore," I said, as I extricated my hand from his grip.

"Naw, you ain't." He ran a hand over his shiny skull. "I could never figure out why Aunt Rachael wanted to name you Albert. You had signs of muscles even when you was a baby. Hell, if she wanted one of them historical names, she ought to have named you Hercules."

Right, I thought, like that would've made my life so much easier.

"Anyway," he continued. "I'm glad you come. Whyn't you grab your stuff and come on inside. I was just about to put supper on the table. I whupped up a mess of pork chops and collard greens . . . I assume livin' up north ain't kilt your taste for home cookin' . . . and I got me a blackberry pie for dessert."

I smiled and wiped at my mouth, afraid the drool would show. My favorite place in DC to eat is called 'Mom's', a soul food joint that prepared food the way people down south have prepared it for a long time, fried in lots of grease—Mom took to using vegetable oil instead of lard in the late 1990s, but is still liberal with it—resulting in mouth-watering dishes that remind me of my childhood. It's not good for cholesterol levels, but, like chicken soup, is great for the soul.

"I've never been known to say no to pork chops and collard greens," I said. "Provided you have cornbread to go with 'em."

"It ain't Thanksgiving or Christmas, so we sure 'nuff ain't gon' be havin' dinner rolls, so cornbread's the only logical choice left."

"Well, just set me a place at the table."

His smile broadened, and he dropped one of his large hands on my shoulder. He didn't squeeze, but I felt the weight of that appendage. I could just imagine what it would feel like if he'd had hostile intent, and winced inwardly. Did I mention that my Cousin Winston weighs over three hundred pounds and is nearly seven feet tall? The fact that he was closer to eighty than seventy didn't make a bit of difference. He was still as intimidating as I remembered from my childhood. His ever-present smile and sunny disposition did nothing to soften that feeling.

"Good to have you here, cousin," he said. "Now, you grab your stuff, and I'll show you where you're bunkin'."

I had no idea how long I'd be in Texas, but had nonetheless packed light. Six pairs of durable and washable pants, four pairs of black cargo pants, one pair of jeans, and one khaki— along with the khaki pants I was wearing, six pair in all—a shirt to go with each pants, black pullovers for the cargo pants, and cotton plaid (red and black) long sleeve shirts for the others, a black nylon jacket just in case it got cool at night and I was outside, and six (seven with what I was wearing) sets of underwear and socks, my black, soft-soled, canvas commando boots, a pair of tattered running shoes, and the black leather slip-on loafers I wore for travel made up most of the black duffel bag. I'd stuffed a toilet kit, my gray cotton running pants and top, and two John Ludlum paperbacks in with the underwear, and that was it. No suit, no ties, and no dress shirts. I had no plans to go anywhere or do anything requiring such attire.

Winston gave me a raised eyebrow when I pulled the duffel from the back seat of the rental.

"I'm assuming you have a washer and dryer?"

"Why, 'course I do," he said, looking slightly offended. "What you think, I'm some kinda backwoods hick who wash his clothes in a big iron pot and hang 'em on a line out back to dry?"

"No, man, I know you live alone, and I wondered if maybe you took your stuff to a laundromat or something."

"That wouldn't be a bad idea, 'ceptin', the closest laundromat's over in Diboll, and it's always crowded. Naw, I got me the latest GE washer and dryer, them energy-saving things that don't use lots of detergent or electricity."

"Well, in that case, I'm good to go. Everything I packed is washable, and I have enough to go a week between washing."

He chuckled. He turned and went back up to the porch, the steps creaking and groaning again. I waited until his bulk was safely on the porch floor before mounting the steps myself. They made hardly a sound as I stepped up.

He led me through the living room, neatly but sparsely furnished, the main feature a large screen television—one of the new model TVs they were coming up with—mounted on the wall in front of a sofa and a reclining chair, and a small desk with a large computer screen and keyboard on top and a bulky CPU on the floor beside it, to the stairs up to the second floor, and down a hall to a bedroom at the end. The big double bed was made up and the room was neat, but it looked like it hadn't been used in a long time. The pink bed spread and the little doilies on the nightstand and bedside chair, though, indicated that it had last been used by a girl or woman. Winston caught my frowning look and laughed.

"This was my baby, Rowena's room," he said. "She the youngest of five, and was the last one to move out. If you don't like that girlie-lookin' bed spread, they's another one in the linen closet in the hall."

I shook my head. "No, this is fine. I don't have any hang ups about stuff like that. Once I'm asleep, I could care less what color the covering is."

I tossed my duffel on the bed and followed him back downstairs to the kitchen.

Unlike the rest of the house, where the furniture was neat, but obviously old and from a time before he lived alone—except for the TV and computer in the living room—the kitchen was new. It was brand spanking new. Gleaming aluminum appliances, granite countertops, an assortment of pots, spatulas, knives and other utensils that would put a five-star restaurant to shame; it was a man's kitchen, a man who not only *liked* to cook, but who knew his way around a stove. It reminded me of my kitchen back home.

I'd put a lot of effort into the kitchen of my old farmhouse near Potomac, Maryland, just outside the District, but I was bush league compared to this. Winston caught me gawking and beamed.

"You like it?"

"Wow!" It was all I could say, but the look on his face told me that it said what he wanted to hear.

"Most of what you see is brand new," he said. "I bought it after my wife, Annie, died. She wouldn't never let me buy new stuff while she was alive. Woman was an okay cook, but for her it was just a job you had to do, and she didn't see spending a lot of money on stoves and pans and such. Me, I like to have the best when I'm cookin'."

"Yeah, I know what you mean. Of course, my kitchen's not nearly as well appointed as yours. This must have cost a bundle."

He shot me a worried—pained—look.

"I heard 'bout your wife and boy. I'm sorry I couldn't get up to Washington for the funeral." He ran his hands over his ample middle. "But, I can't fit in no airplane or bus seat, and I don't like trains. I'd have drove up, but my legs ain't up to that long drive, you know. But, I was there in spirit."

I patted his shoulder.

"I know, I know. No problems, cuz."

"It's been what, ten, twelve years now?"

"It's been fifteen years." I felt the salty sting of unshed tears as I thought about it. "Ethan would be in his twenties now . . . a man."

He gave me a light fist bump to the shoulder. "Hey, I know you done got taught how to cook. How's 'bout you show me you remember how to make cornbread."

"I thought you said you'd already made it."

"I said it was what we oughta have. I ain't said nothin' 'bout it already bein' made. 'Sides, it's got to be fresh baked. You know that. Now, can you do it or not?"

"Get out of my way, and I'll show you."

I actually make a pretty damn good cornbread. My recipe is a variation of what my grandmother taught me.

I mixed a cup of coarse yellow cornmeal and a cup of flour in a medium-sized bowl, and then

I stirred in a teaspoon of salt and two teaspoons of baking powder. Into a little depression in the dry ingredients I broke an egg and used a fork to scramble it up. I filled a cup with buttermilk and poured it slowly into the mixture, stirring until I had a slightly soupy mix, about the consistency of chocolate mousse. There was about an eighth of a cup of milk left—I drank that. Waste not, want not, my grandma always said. That was just about the end of what she'd taught me. The rest of the recipe, except for a half cup of sweet corn, was my own idea. I chopped a white onion and some green peppers into tiny chunks and stirred them, along with the corn, into the cornbread mix. I then stirred in two tablespoons of vegetable oil and poured the mixture into a well-greased loaf pan. That went into the oven that I'd preheated to 325 degrees.

While we waited for the cornbread to bake, Winston and I sat at the kitchen counter with two quart cans of Miller. It's not my favorite beer, but it was ice cold, and my first of the day, so it tasted pretty damn good.

I was just taking my second swig when I noticed that Winston was looking intently at me over the lip of his can. I swallowed and put the can on the table.

"What's on your mind, cousin?" I asked.

He copied me by putting his can on the table. Then, he steepled his large hands and rested his chin on his fingertips. "I was just wondering, Al," he said. "You been a widower for a long time now. You still livin' alone?"

Relatives, even distant cousins, and I was not sure just how distant Winston was, have a tendency to do that—pry into your personal business. At least, the relatives I remembered in

Texas did. There is really no sense of personal space as far as kin is concerned.

"I lived alone for nearly ten years after Sarah and Ethan died. Then, I met someone. She moved in with me a few years back."

"Is it serious?"

"If by that you mean, exclusive, I guess you could call it serious."

"You thinkin' 'bout gettin' hitched?"

Kin or no, it was getting a bit *too* personal for my taste.

"We both value our independence, but enjoy each other's company, so for now, we're just leaving it at that. Why do you ask?"

A flicker of sadness passed across his round face.

"Oh, I don't know. Just thinkin', you know. Annie's been gone comin' up on ten years now, and I been wonderin' whether or not I oughta think about gettin' married again. Rowena, ever time she come home from school . . . she's a junior at Wiley College up in Marshall . . . she bugs me 'bout gettin' a wife to keep me company. You bein' a widower so long, I figured you might have some advice for me."

So, it wasn't just him being curious about my situation. Unfortunately, I wasn't sure I was the person he should be consulting. Sandra and I had been living together for years, and the subject of marriage had never come up. I knew that she was content with the relationship as it was . . . at least, I hoped so . . . and, I wasn't quite ready to take the plunge, because it meant completely letting go of the past, and I wasn't sure I was ready, or able to do that.

"It's nice to have someone to talk to and share things with," I said. "But, marriage is a pretty serious commitment. It's not something you should rush into, and it for damn sure isn't something you should do because someone else recommends it."

He smiled, picked up his beer and took a long swallow. "That's kinda what I been thinkin' myself. Just nice to hear someone in the same boat agree with me." He put the can back down. "Hey, you better check that cornbread. It's probably done by now."

It was. Nice and golden brown on top, and it sprang back when I poked it lightly with my finger. I took it from the oven, and sliced it into squares with a knife from the rack on the counter.

Winston went to the cabinet and removed plates, glasses and utensils and set two places at the square wooden table in the center of the kitchen, and we loaded the plates with golden brown pork chops, mounds of collards, and two squares each of cornbread. He took out a fresh quart of beer and filled the glasses.

There was something comforting about sitting in his kitchen eating the food I remembered from my childhood. We ate in silence. Unlike a lot of people, East Texans don't consider mealtime as a time for conversation. The only sounds were the scraping of forks and knives on the plates and the occasional contented sigh as we washed the food down with beer. After two helpings each of the chops and collards, we had large slices of blackberry pie topped with vanilla ice cream from his industrial-sized freezer.

After supper was finished, I helped him clear the table and then he washed and I dried. We worked in silence; two old bachelors doing after dinner chores.

When the kitchen was done, he took two more beers from the refrigerator and motioned me toward the exit to the living room.

"Let's go set a spell and have an after-dinner beer, and I'll tell you why I asked for your help," he said. "You prefer the living room, or would you like to sit out on the porch?"

It was getting on to 7:00, but the sun was still up. At that time of day in June in DC there would already be a nip in the air, but in East Texas, it was just pleasantly warm. Without the screen on his porch, we'd be eaten alive my mosquitos as big as dragon flies, but I figured the screen would protect us.

"Let's sit on the porch. I haven't done that in a while."

He led the way. His porch furniture, like his kitchen, was new and spotless. Made of bamboo, it was comfortable in the heat, and withstood the humidity well. The mesh screen hummed and clicked to the sound of mosquitos and other flying pests slamming their bodies against it. It was tight enough to keep them out, but clear enough to see through, and the insects swarming in the still warm evening air were a visible cloud roiling beyond it, as were the black shapes knifing through the cloud of insects that I recognized as fruit bats, out of their roosts early, attracted to the sumptuous meal. The sight of the bats feasting on insects reminded me to check and make sure the windows in my bedroom were tightly closed. Evenings can sometimes be uncomfortably warm and some people in the area sleep with windows open. Bats, chasing insects, sometimes fly into those open windows, and if frightened by people awakened by the sound of their wings beating the night air have been known to bite. Cases of rabies from bat bites aren't unknown even in the twenty-first century.

We sat in low-slung chairs on either side of a round table, beers close at hand and he began his story.

"My problem's got to do with land, and to understand it, I have to tell you the history of the place. This here land been in my family since my great-grandpa," he said. "He got forty acres give to him after the War between the States." Like many Texans and other southerners, black and white, he'd been taught that name instead of the Civil War. "Near the end of the war, the rebels was recruiting every man who could walk or hold a shovel to help build fortifications against the northern army. Great-grandpa Levi was drafted by Hood's Division 'n after the war, when Texas was giving rewards to Confederate veterans, they even included the black men. Ever one of 'em got land and even a little pension. 'Course, most of his forty acres was swamp land, but he made a go of it, and was able to buy more until he got it up to 500 acres. It's the biggest black farm in the county, and pretty near the biggest of all. Only old man Jarvis who got a thousand acres next to me, the Woods over in the east part of the county, and the Buford family up north got bigger places, and they all white folks."

"I imagine the other whites around here must resent you for that," I said.

"I 'spect they do, but that don't bother me. I minds my own business, and long's they don't come on my land, I don't give a damn what they think."

"So, it's not the locals giving you land problems?"

He took a sip of beer.

"Not exactly. I mean, young Dudley Jarvis been makin' noises, but he's always been a gasbag, so I ignore him. No, my problem is this white man from Lufkin who been pressuring me for the past two weeks to sell off a hunk of my property."

"Some of your property? I take it this person wants some of your prime acreage?"

"Naw, that's what don't make much sense. He wants the part that's mostly swamp."

"Why would anyone want to buy swamp land?"

"I know, right. He said it was for some kinda scientific research project."

"*What* kind of research project requires that they buy land? Seems to me it would make more sense for them to lease it. Speaking of *them*, who did this guy represent?"

He stood and stretched. "I don't rightly remember, but he give me a card. I'll go fetch it."

A few minutes later he returned clutching a small card in his big mitts. He handed it to me. The name on the card was **Loren Caldwell**, and his title was director of something called **GeoSync**. There was a Lufkin, Texas street address and phone number. It didn't tell me much. With name cards available from online merchants at ten bucks for a hundred, anyone can be anything they choose.

"How much did this Caldwell offer?"

"A hundred thousand dollars for ten acres, and like I said, most of that's swamp land along the creek."

I whistled. I had no idea what Texas farm land was going for, but ten grand per acre sounded like a lot; a lot more than the land was worth, especially for scientific experiments. Loren Caldwell, if indeed that was his real name, was up to something, and I didn't think it had a damn thing to do with science.

"What did you tell him?"

"I told him I'd have to think about it."

"Well, have you . . . thought about it, I mean?"

"Yeah, and I think something stinks about it. I looked up this GeoSync place on my computer, and couldn't find it, so I think this Caldwell fella's some kinda con man. I was about to call him and tell him to forget about it, when that little turd, Dudley Jarvis dropped by and said he'd heard somebody wanted to buy some of my land, and he and his pappy didn't think it was such a good idea. He offered to buy it instead."

My mind was spinning. "Jarvis wants to buy your swamp land?"

"Sho nuff, and he said he'd give me ten thousand more'n Caldwell offered. 'Course, I told him the same thing I told Caldwell. I said I'd have to think about it. That's when I looked you up on my computer and called you."

"You found me through your computer?" He nodded. I sat there with my mouth hanging open. I have a computer . . . in my office, but I can barely use it. I leave the computer stuff to Heather, and here was my elderly cousin living in a one-horse Texas town using a computer to look people up. "You'll have to show me how you did that."

"Rowena showed me how to do it after she bought me one of them PCs. It really ain't all that hard once you get the hang of it, and it's sho nuff handy for looking up crop information and such."

I shook my head. "Winston, you are amazing. So, anyway, you got two people trying to buy a worthless chunk of your land, and I get a feeling you don't want to sell. So, what do you want me to do?"

"Well, I reckon I can take care of Dudley," he said. "But, I don't know what to do about this Caldwell fella. I was kinda hopin' you could figure out what he's really up to."

"Are you seriously considering selling to him?"

He gave me a hard look. "This land been in my family for a long time. It ain't gon' be me what let some stranger come in and take it. Only way any of it be sold is over my dead body, less'n they offer me an amount of money I'd be a fool to turn down." He laughed. "I don't reckon they gon' be doin' that, though."

Chapter 4

We talked a bit longer, but mostly it was him, catching me up on family matters, who died, who got married, and who ran off and joined the army. After he was talked out, we turned in. It was a bit after 10:00 pm. I wanted to call Heather to get her started on tracking Caldwell down, but the hour time difference meant she wasn't in the office, and I had no desire to bother her at home. I did call Sandra to say goodnight just before brushing my teeth and turning in. Our conversation was short. She'd had detention duty at Cabot High School and was bushed, so she'd turned in early. My call had awakened her, and she sounded groggy, so basically I just told her I missed her, loved her, and would call again the next day. She mumbled 'love you, too,' and something else that was too garbled to understand, and I think she'd gone back to sleep while she was breaking the connection.

The next morning, light coming through a gap in the curtains woke me up. I rolled over and peered at my watch on the nightstand. It was 5:30 am, and I was wide awake. Most people get jet lag if they cross three or four time zones, but I don't. Mine is three or less, and the worse is when I do that one-hour shift. My sleep pattern is disrupted for days, and I'm forever forgetting what time it is. Give me a twelve hour shift any day. I knew going back to sleep was out of the question. So, I rolled out of bed, pulled my sweats and sneakers from my duffel, which I'd just kicked into a corner of the bedroom when I came up to go to sleep, and dressed. I left the bedroom and went into the bathroom across the hall, where I splashed cold water on my face and rinsed the acidic taste of stale beer from my mouth, and I instantly regretting doing so. The fluorine and other chemicals that naturally occur in public water supplies in East Texas gives it an oily texture and a metallic taste. It's harmless, in fact, the fluorine is good for keeping teeth strong and healthy, but it takes some getting used to.

I eased down the stairs, trying not to make any noise, but as I reached the bottom, I heard a rattling sound coming from the kitchen.

Winston, dressed in the same overalls, but with a faded denim shirt on, stood at the counter near the stove filling three large thermos jugs with coffee from a big aluminum pot.

"Mornin', Al," he said. "You up early."

"Yeah, I thought I'd get in a run before breakfast. You're up pretty early yourself."

"Hey, this a farm, you know. When they say get up with the chickens, it ain't no joke 'round here. Got to get the cows milked and the chickens fed and watered, or I got problems. You ain't heard a ruckus until you got a barn full of un-milked cows. A full udder, I'm told by the vet, is pretty danged painful."

I'd just have to take his word for that.

"Do you do all that yourself?"

"Naw, I got me two Mexican guys workin' for me. They live the other side of town, but work for me five days a week." He pointed to the thermos jugs. "They eat breakfast 'fore they come to work, but they like my coffee, so I make a jug for each of 'em."

I'd forgotten what life was like on a farm. Up with the sun, work all day, and pray for rain. Oh, and no retirement plan, which explained my elderly cousin being up so early.

"If you need me to help, I'll be happy to after my run," I said.

"That's okay. Juan and Diego can take care of it. I don't have to do too much myself anymore, but I like to keep my hand in." He tucked one of the jugs under his arm and grabbed the other two, one in each hand, and headed for the back door. "You want a good run," he said. "I recommend you go down the drive to the main road, take a right and run down to the end of the fence line and back. According to Donald, my oldest, that's 'xactly four miles. He in the Air Force stationed down in San Antone, and when he come visit, he run four mile every day." He walked out the door shaking his head and looking bemused.

I understood that. I was in the habit of jogging four miles because that had been the distance we were required to run when I was in the army. No one ever explained why four miles; I figured some general had probably chosen the distance at random. Whatever the reason, the four-mile run was the military standard. It made about as much sense as some of the people in Texas being part of the crowd objecting to adding fluoride to water because they feared it was part of a Communist plot to poison Americans, when the chemical occurred naturally in our water supply, and as far as I knew, the only thing poisoning people in East Texas was the rotgut moonshine they drank and the tobacco they dipped, chewed and smoked, which tended after a few decades to undercut the advantages of the fluorine in the water.

The smell of sweat, dried animal dung, and laundry detergent that pervaded Winston's house—the bedroom in which I slept, though, bore the flowery smell of potpourri from the little bags of the stuff in the drawer of the nightstand—told me that he, like me, wasn't a smoker; that and his clean, but slightly crooked teeth.

I followed Winston out the back door. That smell of animal waste, not all that unpleasant really, hung in the warm morning air. I stood on the back porch for a few minutes, stretching my muscles. When they felt loose enough, I hopped off the porch and began jogging around the side of the house. Winston, followed by a short, slight, brown-skinned man, was just entering the dairy barn. He looked over his shoulder and waved at me. I waved back.

Despite the early hour, the air was warm, and I began sweating as soon as I started running. The path from the house to the road was red clay, and my running kicked up a fine cloud of red dust which stuck to my exposed skin. It was better once I reached the road— marginally, in that there was less dust, and thanks to the earliness, no cars for me to dodge. I was drenched and coated in a thin layer of sticky wet mud by the time I'd done the whole four miles to the end of the fence line and back to the back porch. Winston and two brown-skinned men who looked like twins were coming out of one of the long, low chicken houses. I was doing my wind-down stretching when the three of them approached.

"Man, you look like one of them Injun Ghost Dancers," Winston said. "Whyn't you go up and wash off, and I'll get breakfast started. Oh, by the way, this here's Juan and Diego Martinez, they're brothers and my hired hands; boys, this is my cousin Al Pennyback, come down from Washington, DC."

Their heads bobbed in unison. *"Con much gusto,"* said the one on Winston's left. "Please to meet you, *senor*," the one on his right said. I returned their nods.

"I need a shower in the worst way," I said. "I forgot about this red dirt and how it sticks to everything."

"You'll get used to it in a couple days. Well, come on boys, let's go back to the dairy barn and wash up for breakfast."

They walked away and I entered the kitchen after knocking off as much of the dust and slurry as possible. I made my way carefully through the house and to the second floor, trying to avoid leaving a trail of red slime in my wake.

Thirty minutes later, after a thorough scrub-down, I was feeling almost human and dressed in jeans, one of my black commando shirts, and the black jungle boots. Downstairs, I found Winston at the stove and his two hired hands sitting at the kitchen table with cups of steaming coffee between their mitts. The aroma of fried meat and fresh bread was thick in the air.

"Pull up a chair," Winston said. "I'm just scrambling some eggs. They'll be ready in a minute."

I nodded at the table, and got two heads bobbing back at me, and then walked to the stove and watched over his shoulder as Winston broke a dozen eggs into a bowl and then added chopped fresh green onion, green chili peppers, chunks of cheddar cheese, and two tablespoons of buttermilk, which stirred in well. He then poured the eggs into a big iron skillet and used a spatula to stir it around until it was a fluffy mass that made my mouth water.

Winston smiled at me as he ladled scrambled eggs onto four plates, followed by two biscuits, a thick slice of ham and a small mound of home fried potatoes on each plate. He put plates in front of Juan and Diego who made half-hearted noises about having already eaten, but then began digging into the food. He put the other two in front of the two empty chairs and motioned me to the one facing the window. I copied the Martinez's and began to demolish the food, while Winston went back to the sink and got the coffee pot and four cups. He filled the cups and put one by each plate and the pot in the center of the table.

"I'd say eat up," he said. "But, you three done already ate most of your food, so I'll just say enjoy." He took a sip of coffee and then began eating. Compared to the three of us he was a dainty eater.

There was no more conversation until all the food was gone and Winston and the two hired men went out to finish chores. I poured myself a second cup of coffee and went into the living room where I hit Sandra's number on my speed dial.

She answered on the first ring. "Al, darling, did you call me last night?"

"Yeah, babe," I said. "Sorry for calling so late, but I got caught up with my cousin. You sounded out of it."

"I was. You know how it is at the end of the school year. With less than a week left until summer vacation starts, even the star students make trouble. I had detention duty, which wasn't too bad . . . only had to break up three fights . . . but, enough of my problems, what's going on with your cousin?"

I gave her the condensed version of what Winston had told me.

"So, what do you plan to do to help him?" she asked.

"I guess my first task will be to find out who this Caldwell is and who he represents."

"I think you're right. He sounds fishy. No school or research firm buys land for experiments. It's cheaper to rent it, and they lowball the rent."

That's along the lines I'd been thinking myself, only she as a teacher would know more about it than me.

"Anyway, I'm gonna get Heather to track this guy down. Maybe then I can find out what he's really up to."

There was a long silence. I could hear my own heartbeats. "When are you coming home?" she asked.

"Couple of days I'd think. This doesn't seem all that complicated. My cousin's wife died a few years ago, and his last kid just went off to college. I think he was just lonely and reached out to me for company."

"Texas to Washington is a long way to reach, babe." She laughed, but there was a brittle tone to her laughter.

"You know Texans have no sense of scale," I said. "Something about living in the second biggest state. Anyway, I miss you."

"Miss you too."

"Love ya, babe."

Another pause. "I love you too, Al Pennyback. Now, you hurry and get your ass home."

I heard a little of the old fire then.

"You got it, Sandra Winter, and you keep your ass warm."

"I'd rather have you here to warm it for me."

All the fire was back now,

"Looking forward to it, babe. See ya soon."

We broke the connection at the same time; a little technique we'd developed over time so neither of us had to be hanging up on the other. Silly, I know, but when you're in love, you do silly things.

I hit number two on my speed dial. Heather let it ring three times before answering. "Hey, boss man, what's up? How's the weather in the Lone Star state?"

"Hot, muggy, and I'm ready to come home," I said. "How're things on the home front?"

"Clients beating down the door; can't you hear the noise? Seriously, I'm sitting here staring at a cobweb in the corner, and wondering why the spider abandoned it."

"Well, I have a little job for you."

I heard the rustle of paper. "Thank you," she said. "What is it?"

I told her to track down Loren Caldwell and who he really worked for, determine if GeoSync was for real, and as an afterthought, do a background check on Winston's neighbor, Dudley Jarvis.

"Shoot," she said. "That won't take more than an hour or so. I'm bored, Al. I need a challenge, some *real* work."

"Okay, how about this; look up land prices for this part of Texas, and tell me if ten thousand dollars an acre for swamp land makes sense."

"That's more like it. I'll get back to you as soon as I have something."

Just as I broke the connection, I heard a commotion from the front of the house. I got up and crossed the living room and pulled the front door open.

Winston was standing at the bottom steps with his hands on his hips. The Martinez brothers flanked him. Facing them was a gaunt, red-faced man with lank brown hair that covered his ears. He wore faded jeans and a red long-sleeved shirt. At least a foot shorter than Winston, he had to tilt his head back to look up at him.

Charles Ray

Chapter 5

Standing there, glaring up at Winston, Dudley
Jarvis wasn't much to look at. His face was
reddish from a lot of time in the unrelenting
East Texas sun, but with an underlying grayish
pallor. He had the bloodshot, watery blue eyes
and the red lines of veins on the end of his nose
of a heavy drinker. He looked to be my age, but
with the leathery skin covering his face and
hands it was hard to pin his age down with any
specificity. Tiny spider web lines radiated from
the corners of his eyes. His voice, when he
spoke, had the nasally, lazy twang typical of
East Texans, not quite the hokey drawl you
hear on TV shows purporting to show typical
Texans, and not quite the slow sing-song mish-
mash of a true southerner; more of a poor
mashup of both that grated on the ears and
made you want to scream.

"Now, you listen to me, Winston," he said.
"Me 'n pa done treated you good, ain't we? No

different than we'd treat a white man. We know you thinkin' 'bout takin' that Caldwell fella's offer, and frankly we don't cotton to no stranger hornin' in on the land 'round here."

"You don't know nothin', Dudley Jarvis; you sho nuff don't know what I'm thinkin'." A vein in Winston's neck pulsated, and his large hands were clenched so tightly his knuckles were yellowish-gray against the dark skin of the rest of his hand.

I pushed the screen door open and stepped forward onto the top step and a bit to Winston's right so that Jarvis could see me. His eyes narrowed to slits as I stepped from the shadow of the porch.

"Who is this? Some flunky Caldwell sent out to help talk you into sellin'? You work for Caldwell, boy?"

I started forward, but Winston held a hand up, blocking me. He turned and frowned at me, shaking his head.

"This here's my cousin, come down from Washington, DC to visit me," he said. "And, you don't be callin' him boy." There was steel in his voice. Jarvis took a step back, and the gray pallor was more pronounced.

"Sorry, no offense meant," he said. "So, you Winston's northern cousin come to visit, eh? What you think of our fair town?"

"Not much, really," I said. "I thought Texas was an old Indian word that meant friendly, but I'm not getting any friendly vibes at the moment."

Several expressions flickered across his face; confusion, a tinge of anger, and then a wolfish smile.

"Come on, Winston, you ain't gon' git a better offer than what me 'n pa givin' you."

"I done told you, Dudley Jarvis," Winston said in a tight voice. "My land ain't for sale, to nobody for *no* price."

Jarvis's gaze shifted from Winston to me and back again. "I wish't I could trust what you say, Winston, truly I do. But, I know men like Caldwell. He gon' keep dangling dollar signs in front of your eyes 'till you can't resist. I can't let that happen . . . me'n pa can't."

I stepped forward to stand beside my cousin. This time Winston didn't try to stop me.

"Why are you so concerned about the sale of property that doesn't belong to you?" I asked.

He shot me an irritated glare.

"Not that it's any of your business, but 'round these parts we don't cotton to strangers movin' in."

There was a certain sense to that. Small East Texas towns, at least in my recollection, tend toward exclusivity. If you're not born there, you'll always be an outsider, or, as in my case, if you leave you're viewed as a traitor. But, there was something else. I couldn't quite put my finger on it, but something . . . maybe it was the tension in his voice . . . something else was going on.

"Do you know Caldwell?" I asked.

"Naw, and I don't need to. He's an outsider."

"Yeah, but the land he wants to buy is worthless swampland. You can't grow anything on it." I looked at Winston, who nodded. "So, what does it matter if it's sold?"

As I mentioned the land, he blinked rapidly three times and a muscle in his cheek twitched; a brief tic that would have gone unnoticed in a normal conversation. But, I was watching him closely, watching his expressions and body language, which often provide more information than words. There was something about the land that bothered him. If I only knew what.

"It's like I done said. We don't cotton to havin' a stranger come in and buy up land next to us. You let 'em get a toe in the door, and pretty soon, they've taken over the whole house. Now, Winston here, his family been here for three generations. We used to that. We don't know this fella Caldwell, or what he represents, and me and pa don't want him comin' in here."

"It's my land," Winston said. "What I decide to do with it ain't no concern of yours."

Jarvis blew air through his nose noisily.

"It's too bad you see it that way, Winston. I was hopin' you'd be reasonable."

"What's that supposed to mean?" I asked.

He glared at me, opened his mouth as if to speak, and then snapped it shut. Without a further word, he turned on his heel and strode to the fire engine red Dodge Ram pickup parked behind my rental. He shot us a dirty look as he pulled himself up into the cab. Then, he slammed the door, started the engine, backed up, and gunned the engine, throwing a cloud of dust and gravel our way as he raced toward the road.

After his truck made a tire-screeching right turn onto the road, I turned to Winston.

"What the hell was that about?"

"I be doggone if I know," he said. "I was born in this house, and lived here my whole life, and in all that time, I 'spect I done spoke to Dudley Jarvis maybe two, three times a year, and I ain't never spoke to his daddy; in fact, I ain't even seen him for the past four or five years. I ain't got no idea why they'd be so het up 'bout somebody wantin' to buy some of my land."

"I know you said you could take care of him, but I'd like to dig a bit and see if I can find out why."

He shrugged. "You can if you want to, but I think it's like he said, him and his daddy don't want no strangers movin' in. They like that, them Jarvis's is, ain't never been to friendly with nobody."

"Could be, but I think there's more to it than that."

Charles Ray

Chapter 6

Winston wasn't convinced that Jarvis was up to anything shady, but my gut told me he was, and I learned a long time ago to trust my gut. Checking up on him, though, was second on my list of things to do. He was a minor irritant, a puzzle in need of a solution, while Caldwell was the main problem.

"I'll save Jarvis and his father for later," I said. "First thing I need to do is drive up to Lufkin and visit Mr. Caldwell. I'd like to get a sense of him."

He turned to the Martinez brothers. "You fellas go on back and finish seein' to the chickens, and I'll be out to help you directly," he said. Then he turned and faced me. "You ain't gotta go all the way to Lufkin to talk to him. He said he'd be stayin' here in Poseyville 'till I made up my mind. He at the Bide a While Motel."

He gave me directions to the place, but in a town as small as Poseyville, it wouldn't have taken me long to find it by just driving aimlessly around. The town had one main street, the U.S. 64 bypass which was appropriately named Main Street, and three cross streets, Oak, Pine, and Sycamore. The Bide a While Motel, Winston had informed me, was on Sycamore, at the south end of town.

The first thing I saw as I drove into what passed for downtown Poseyville was the two gas stations, one on either side of the street. No matter how small the town in Texas, there will always be a gas station or two to serve the trucks and farm vehicles in the nearby area, and despite being in the state where the bulk of the big oil companies have a presence, the price of a gallon of gas rivals some of the rural areas in Virginia and Maryland. In Poseyville's case, the refineries of Houston are less than 200 miles away, just a short drive up U.S. 59 or 69, so you'd think the prices would be significantly lower. That makes about as much sense to me as seeing different prices for a gallon of the same brand of fuel at stations only a few miles apart.

Next to the gas station on the right was a two-story brick building, a boarded up movie theater whose sagging marque advertised 'Patton,' with George C. Scott, a movie from 1970. A tree grew out of a gap in the brick wall on the building's right, and I would bet that raccoons, snakes and other wildlife had taken up residence in its darkened innards. Across from the abandoned theater was a hardware store. It was hard to tell from the darkened windows if it, too, was a business that had bone belly up or not. Next was a dry good store, a 'Five and Dime' that sold curios and odds and ends, a drug store, and across from it a restaurant, 'Bob's BBQ.' All of the buildings were made of red brick, their sides all soot-stained and mold-covered, and looking as if a good shove would reduce them to piles of rubble. Clearly, Poseyville's business district had seen better days.

Looking down Oak and Pine as I passed the intersections, I saw more dingy looking brick buildings and the occasional wood frame house, probably the dwelling of one of the town merchants. Most of the official population of Poseyville lived on the surrounding farms which added to the ghost town atmosphere of the place. I wouldn't have been surprised to see an old guy sitting on an overturned crate whittling and chewing tobacco—I didn't, but it would have surprised me.

The town's sole traffic light was at the intersection of Main and Sycamore Streets, and it was red, and it took its own sweet time to change to green. I hung a left onto Sycamore, and entered a different Poseyville.

At the corner of Main and Sycamore was a white building, made of poured concrete that looked like it had a fresh coat of paint. A large brass sign on the building identified its occupants as the Poseyville City Hall, Mayor's Office, Police and Fire Departments. Next to that was a squat building that hadn't been painted in a while, with green and gray stains on the walls and bars on the windows and a sign over the entrance identifying it as the Poseyville Jail. It sat across from the First Mercantile Bank. The bank was made of red brick, but didn't look derelict at all. A Kwik Mart grocery set well back from the street was next to the bank, and next to it was the

Bide a While Motel and Conference Center. It was a two-story structure of white stone with a green tile roof and a large plastic and steel sign festooned with neon lights that probably lit the whole block at night. Urban renewal had come to at least one block of Poseyville. No, strike that; urban renewal had come to only *one* of Poseyville's city blocks. The rest of the town had been left to molder in the 1970s.

I pulled into the parking lot in front of the motel. It was large enough for about fifty cars, but there were only five occupied spaces, and my guess was that at least one if not more of those were staff, not guests. I parked in a space not far from the reception entrance.

The lobby was a clone of motel lobbies anywhere in the country. White tile floor, plastic ferns in large plastic urns flanking a laminated desk with black faux marble top behind which stood a thin-faced woman with a flat chest and big hair, wearing a blue blazer and a pasted-on smile; her watery blue eyes widened as I approached her.

"Uh, good mornin', sir," she said. "How can I help y'all?"

"I'm looking for Loren Caldwell," I said. "I understand he's staying here?"

The tension in her face eased. She tapped a few keys on the keyboard on the counter and looked at a small video screen sitting beside it. "Why yes, we do have a Mr. Caldwell registered."

I knew it would do no good, even in a one-horse town like Poseyville, to ask for his room number. Even the cops need a warrant to make hotel staff provide information like that.

"Could you please ring his room and ask him if I could talk to him?"

"Oh, no need for that. He's rented one of our conference rooms to use as a makeshift office while he's here in Poseyville." She pointed. "It's down that hallway over there. Second door on your right. Y'all just go right on in."

The hallway was covered by a thin green carpet with gold trim. The first door on my left was the exercise room, which was across from the business center. The second door on the right had a brass plaque that read, 'Sam Houston Conference Room.' Beneath that was a cardboard rectangle with 'GeoSync – Poseyville Office' written on it with a black marker. I pulled the door open and stepped inside.

The gold-trim green carpet continued inside. I entered a shallow space, a small desk, behind which sat a redhead whose hair was pulled back into a small bun, the first woman I'd seen so far who didn't have a big Dolly Parton-like hairdo. The dark blue jacket she wore strained to hold her generous bosom. She was attractive, despite the crows' feet emanating from the corners of her eyes, probably somewhere in her mid- to late-forties. On her left were two plastic chairs flanking a cheap looking Chinese vase containing a plastic fern. Behind her was one of those portable walls that hotels use to break large spaces up into smaller spaces, only this one had a door in it a few feet to her right. She looked up and smiled at me over the top of her gold-rimmed spectacles.

"Good morning, welcome to GeoSync. How may I help you?" Her voice was bright and perky, and she sounded younger than she looked. And, I liked it that she didn't use the plural, 'y'all.'

A lot more welcoming than the receptionist had been. But, I suppose, since I'd gotten past her I was considered a potential customer for whatever Caldwell was selling, and not just some nosy stranger who wandered in off the street.

"Is Mr. Caldwell available?" I asked.

"Yes, he is," she said. "May I ask your name and the nature of your business?"

"My name is Al Pennyback, and I'm a relative of Winston Jones," I said. "Mr. Caldwell offered to buy a piece of Mr. Jones's property, and Mr. Jones asked me to handle the discussions relating to it." I debated showing her my PI card, and then decided against it. There's something about private investigators that causes a lot of people to freeze up and become uncooperative; guilty consciences or what, I don't know, but when I absolutely didn't have to, I often neglected to tell people what I did for a living.

She kept the thousand-watt smile on her porcelain face as she held up a well-manicured finger in a 'hold on a minute' gesture. She picked up the phone, pushed the intercom button and tole whoever answered my name and reason for visiting, bobbing her head up and down as she spoke. She listened for a few seconds, still smiling up at me. Then, she put the phone down and waved her hand toward the door to her right.

"Go right on through, Mr. Pennyback; Mr. Caldwell will see you."

Her voice was like that of a flight attendant in first class. She had experience as a gatekeeper for important people, but people who needed to make a good impression on visitors, and Caldwell obviously had enough money, clout, or both, to be able to rent a whole conference room and then have it reconfigured to his convenience. If this was a con, the guy had invested a significant amount in it. That meant there was a big potential payoff down the road. That's the skeptic in me talking. It's not that I don't trust people—the fact is, I *don't* trust most people because they've given me tons of valid reasons not to—it's that when something smells like a fish, it's usually a fish, and even before I met Caldwell, his operation smelled like a three-day-old fish.

The door opened inward onto a huge space. A large executive desk sat facing the door. Behind it was a large corkboard about six feet high and at least ten feet wide. Two maps were affixed to the corkboard with red thumbtacks; one was a map of the United States with an irregular blue shape bisecting the country north to south right through the middle, and the other was a topographical map of Texas with a big green tack stuck in it right about where I'd guess Poseyville was.

Caldwell sat in a big leather executive chair behind the desk, which was littered with papers. He wore a white shirt with the sleeves rolled up to his elbows and the top button undone and his tie hanging loosely. His jacket hung over the back of one of the two chairs at the left side of his desk.

As I approached the desk, he stood. He wasn't skinny, and he wasn't fat, but he had the start of a beer belly straining at the waist of his gray pants. His face was narrow with a sharp nose that stuck out like a bird's beak, and a hairline that started at the top of his narrow skull. He'd made a vain effort to comb his lank brown hair over the bald spot, but only succeeded in drawing more attention to it.

He thrust out his right hand and beamed at me. "Mr. Pennyback, welcome. I'm Loren Caldwell, representing GeoSync, a geological research firm. Have a seat. So, you're representing Mr. Jones. Are you a lawyer?"

All this was said in a machine gun staccato as he shook my hand and guided me to the chair that didn't have his coat on it. I don't know many scientists, but he didn't strike me as the scientific type. He came across more like a carnival barker or a used car salesman.

"No, I'm not a lawyer," I said after I'd settled myself on the chair. "But, Cousin Winston's not a well-educated man, and he felt I might be better able to evaluate your offer."

The smile stayed plastered on his face, but his eyes weren't smiling, and he leaned back in his chair and regarded me down his beak of a nose.

"Well, I guess getting a second opinion makes sense," he said. "Of course, there's not much to think about. We're offering your cousin a hundred thousand dollars for what's essentially useless land."

"Which brings up an interesting question, Mr. Caldwell; if the land's so useless, why are you willing to pay so much for it?"

"Ah," he said, smiling. "I should have made myself clearer. The land's useless for farming, but for my organization it's a gold mine . . . a scientific gold mine."

"In what way?"

He pointed to the U.S. Map. "I don't know if you're aware of it, Mr. Pennyback, but a hundred million years ago, during the Cretaceous Period, North America was split by an inland sea that was 2,000 miles long and 600 miles wide. What is now the state of Texas was completely submerged under water that was 2,500 feet deep in some places. That sea disappeared 35 to 55 million years ago." He turned back to me, steepled his hands and rested his chin on his fingertips. "Swamp areas like that on your cousin's property were once under water. Studying them gives us a picture of the earth during that time."

I wasn't aware of that, but then, my interest in history was pretty much restricted to the periods that had people who could write about it. Unlike a lot of kids, dinosaurs never did it for me. What I was aware of, though, was that he sounded like he was reciting a script that he'd spent a lot of time memorizing. It was a case of too much information or too technical nature that a layman like me wouldn't understand or be interested in, so why even bother giving it to me in the first place. If he'd been for real, he would've given me a dumbed-down, abbreviated version, and said it slowly to make sure my feeble, non-scientific brain could absorb it. Throwing all the techno-babble at me was a way of intimidating me by impressing the hell out of me. It wasn't working.

"So, you're an archeologist? You want to dig in that swamp looking for relics?"

The look he gave me was almost withering. "No, I'm a geologist, but, yes, we do plan to dig, and I suppose you could say we're looking for relics, but relics of the geological kind."

Now, I was getting into the area of the two Ps, puzzled and pissed. I didn't know jack about an inland sea, but I did know that digging holes in a swamp is like pissing into a big wind, it gets you nowhere.

"How do you dig holes in the swamp and find anything? I mean, we're talking about a sea almost half a mile deep; you have to go way down, don't you?"

Now, he was looking at me like I was the only kid in class who didn't know the answer to 'what's two plus two.' "The swamp, the water-saturated earth, in that area only goes down about ten feet or so. Below that is hard pan, and since this area was near the eastern shore of the sea, we only have to go down a few hundred feet to get to the strata we're interested in."

"Okay, I'll take your word for that," I said, not taking his word for anything. "But why buy the land, and at such a price? Wouldn't it make more sense to rent it?"

His brow wrinkled and he stared at me. "You sure you're not a lawyer, Mr. Pennyback?"

"Pretty sure," I said. "So, what's your answer to that?"

"Uh, I'll have to confer with my bo-, colleagues in Lufkin and get back to you on that."

I stood and stuck out my hand; a phony smile plastered on my face.

"Look forward to hearing from you then, Mr. Caldwell."

Charles Ray

Chapter 7

On my way back to Winston's place, I stopped at Bob's BBQ and picked up three racks of barbecue ribs, two pounds of pulled pork, and two pounds of spicy sausage; my contribution to the larder, and because I have a major addiction to barbecue. The guy behind the counter was also tending the big brick grill upon which several yards of pork ribs, sausages and chicken parts were giving off aromas that burned my eyes and made my mouth water at the same time.

Bob's was a traditional barbecue joint; uneven wooden planks threatened to trip you as you crossed the floor from the entrance, threading your way between square, four-person tables covered in brown butcher paper. Paper plates and stacks of old newspapers covered one end of the glass-front counter, inside which were loaves of bread that was sliced right before your eyes to make pulled pork or link sausage sandwiches. A cloud of gray smoke billowed off the grill and created a second, gauzy ceiling. The wooden walls were covered in graffiti and grease. A place like Bob's, if it was in DC, would be closed down as a health hazard. I pitied the foolish safety inspector who tried to shut one down in rural Texas. He'd be lucky if all they did to him was tar and feather him and ride him out of town tied to a railroad tie. Yeah, barbecue served traditional style ranks behind guns, pickups, and football in the Lone Star State, and was about the only thing that ever really made me want to come back.

When I got back to Winston's place, it looked like he had company. There was a yellow Prius parked behind his pickup. I pulled in behind it. Lugging over eight pounds of meat in three large packages, I made it to the top of the steps, but couldn't quite manage the screen door, so I kicked on it until the front door opened.

"What the hell's all this noise," a deep, resonant female voice demanded. A short woman wearing faded jeans that accented her plump thighs that rubbed together when she moved, wide hips, and a yellow tee shirt that stretched over her ample breasts, stepped through the door.

"I've got a handful and can't get the screen door open," I said.

She stepped closer to the screen door and I got a closer look. Her hair was shiny black and close to her skull. She had a round face with prominent cheekbones and large brown eyes. She wore no makeup and had a reasonably attractive face, except for the way her fleshy lips turned down in a frown.

"Who the hell are you, and why are you banging on our door?"

When she snarled, I noticed the prominent space between her two front teeth and the slight resemblance to Winston.

"You must be Rowena, Winston's daughter," I said.

"What if I am? You still haven't told me who you are."

She was right. I hadn't. There was something about standing there on the steps with my arms full of meat that had thrown me off stride.

"I'm Al Pennyback, and if you *are* Rowena, I guess that makes me your cousin a time or two removed, or something."

The expression on her face changed from pissed off to puzzled to a tentative smile, to a beaming grin that made her face look even prettier. No, except for the gap between her two front teeth, she didn't look like Winston at all—thank goodness. I like my cousin, but he won't win any beauty contests, unless there's a 'Beast' category.

"Al Pennyback, from the Pennybacks who used to live up in Shelby County? Oh my goodness, you're daddy's cousin from Washington." She pushed the door open, almost toppling me from the steps. "Daddy said you'd come down, but that you'd gone into town to take care of some business. He didn't know what time you were coming back. Oh, listen to me, running on. You need to get that meat in the kitchen. Come on in."

She did run on. Another difference between her and Winston. He talked when he had something to say, and kept his mouth shut when he didn't. I remembered that it was another thing I liked about him when I was a kid, he didn't have to be talking all the time.

I squeezed past her and when I entered the porch, she grabbed the sack of ribs from me.

"Man, that barbecue certainly smells good. So, you're the one daddy's always talking about?"

"I suppose so," I said. "Although, I don't know what he could be saying about me, this is the first time I've seen him since shortly before I graduated from high school, and we are *not* gonna talk about how long ago that was."

"Oh, he's always talking about Little Al did this, and Little Al did that," she said over her shoulder as she led me into the house. "After I bought him that computer, hooked it up to the Internet and taught him how to use it, he's been reading all kinds of stuff on line, and he found you there. I guess you were some kind of war hero or something?"

"I was in the army, but I'm not sure I'd call myself a war hero."

"You are according to daddy." She stopped at the kitchen door and turned to face me, eying me from head to foot. "Although, I don't see anything little about you, so I don't know why he's always calling you Little Al."

"Well, I was a bit of a runt until I got my growth spurt in junior high school. We didn't see much of each other after that, and, of course, he's so much bigger than me, so I guess he just remembers the little runt."

She chuckled. "Well, you sure aren't a runt anymore." She turned and walked into the kitchen. After putting the ribs on the kitchen counter, she turned and leaned back against it. "You married?"

"Uh, no, I'm not."

"Got a girlfriend?"

There was that East Texas 'in your business' again. Maybe if I stayed long enough I'd get used to it. Then again, I never liked it when I was a kid, so there was about as much chance of that as a snowball rolling through hell and not losing weight. But, I was taught to be polite, and she was kin after all.

"Yeah, I do."

She nodded her head as if to say, 'okay, that'll do.'

"Whatcha got in the other bags? It sure smells good."

"Pulled pork and sausage," I said. "I wanted to repay Winston for the great dinner he cooked last night."

"Why don't you put the pork and sausage in the fridge, and I'll whip up some potato salad and corn on the cob for supper. We can have the sausage for breakfast and the pork for another time."

"You need any help?" I asked.

"Nah, I can handle it. I've been doing most of the cooking for daddy since mama died."

If she was as good as her father, she was a good cook, and the expression on her face said she didn't think I'd be anything but in the way in the kitchen. I needed to do some thinking about the situation anyway, so I decided not to argue with her.

"By the way, I think your dad put me in your room. I should probably move my things to one of the other bedrooms."

"No need," she said. "You hadn't even unpacked, so I moved your stuff to the room next to mine. And, don't worry, I made the bed for you and put in some extra towels in the bathroom. We'll be sharing it, and I don't know about you, but I don't like to use towels someone else's been using."

I'm the same way. Sandra and I, for instance, share a bed, but we never—I mean never—use each other's towels. To me, that's akin to sharing a toothbrush.

"Not a problem, Rowena. Do you know where Winston is right now?"

He's in the tool house. That's the small house just behind the first chicken shed. You can't miss it."

"I think I'll change clothes and go help him do chores."

Her eyebrows rose and she cocked her head as she looked at me with a half-smile on her face.

"You ever do any farming . . . Little Al?"

"Of course not," I said. "We lived in town when I was a kid, and when I left home, I joined the army. But, what does that have to do with anything? Farming can't be all that difficult."

One of her brows dipped, and the other arched even higher. Hands on ample hips, feet spread, she smiled at me, looking like a caramel-colored pixie. "Okay, Cousin Al, you go ahead and change and go on and help daddy with his . . . simple chores."

With a dismissive shrug, she turned back to the counter and began peeling potatoes, whistling a tuneless song.

Charles Ray

Chapter 8

I don't like to think about what happened next. That's the way the mind works, when you screw up, you try to forget it. You see it on TV shows, traumatic experiences are mentally blocked. Don't you believe it. You screw up, and you'll remember it forever— unless someone came close to killing you. That's some scary shit, and you might, just might, block that out. The rest of it, though, nah; those screw ups just rattle around your brain until your brain stops firing.

I changed into jeans and a wrinkled plaid shirt after unpacking and hanging my stuff in the bedroom adjacent to the one I'd been evicted from. I then went out through the kitchen, suffering Rowena's giggles as I passed her, to find Winston working with a wicked-looking piece of machinery outside the tool shed.

He said it was a cultivator. I had no idea what a cultivator was, but it looked dangerous, with circular wheels with curved blades around them, each blade big enough and sharp enough to slice your hand off like a hot knife through a stick of butter. And,

Winston had his arms buried in that wicked looking tangle of sharp metal up to his elbows as he worked with a screwdriver to 'adjust the blade angle.' I decided to watch instead of offering my help, and it was the longest hour of my life. I flinched every time he moved his hand, certain he was about to lose it.

But, he didn't. He got the 'angle adjusted' to his satisfaction and manhandled the cultivator back into the tool shed which contained several other pieces of equipment, among which I only recognized a multi-blade plow, and a tractor. His tool 'shed,' by the way, was about the size of a ten-car garage, and it was crammed from corner to corner with various and sundry farm implements, tools, and vehicles, some of them looking like they came from an Inquisition torture chamber.

So much for farming being simple.

After he'd finished his work on the tools, Winston summoned the Martinez brothers, and told them to wash up and join us for supper. The five of us ate barbecued ribs, potato salad, baked beans, and fresh-baked cornbread, washed down with iced tea in the big dining room. After the Martinez's had thanked Rowena effusively for the meal that was *muy delicioso* and departed, Winston, Rowena and I grabbed quarts of Pabst Blue Ribbon beer and retired to the front porch. They sat on either side of me.

For a while, we just sat and listened to the chirping, clicking and whirring of the early evening dragonflies, mosquitos and cicadas, and the whoosh of the bats' wings as they dive-bombed their melodious evening meals, sipping occasionally from the tall cans and making contented 'aah' sounds.

Finally, Winston broke the silence. "What'd you find out from that Caldwell fella, Al?" he asked.

"Not much, I'm afraid. I think he told me the same thing he told you." I explained the bit about digging for geological artifacts in what was once an inland sea.

"That makes no sense," Rowena said.

We both looked at her. She stared back.

"What?" she said.

"Care to explain why it makes no sense?" I said.

She put her beer on the small table between us and twisted around in her chair to face me, raising a finger.

"For one thing, why would they want swamp land to dig in? If this area's part of that inland sea they told you about, the dry land next to the swamp would be easier to dig in." She held up a second finger. "Number two, why do they want to buy the land; and way over market value at that? I don't know of any research outfit with that kind of money unless they work for the government."

What she said made sense, but I had to play devil's advocate.

"What if they work for some big company?" I asked.

She snorted. "What big company do you know pays for worthless land? And, I don't know of any big companies that give a damn about science unless they can make money from it. How is knowing what life was like millions of years ago gonna make a company money?"

Winston grunted. "You know, Rowena's right. It don't make no sense. If they gon' dig down in that holler, they gon' have to wear gas masks."

"Huh?" I said.

"How do you know that, daddy?" Rowena asked. "You said you never went down there."

He looked sheepish.

"Uh, well, I said that so you children wouldn't go wanderin' into that swamp. I went down there once, when I was 'bout fourteen, I guess. My daddy tanned my hide good for it, and I never went back. 'Course, that place scared me so, I wouldna gone back even if he hadn't whupped me."

"I guess a swamp can be pretty scary at night," I said.

"Yeah, but this one's scary night and day 'cause it's hainted."

Rowena was taking a drink and she sputtered beer from her mouth and nose. When she'd recovered from a coughing fit, she looked wide-eyed at her father.

"Daddy, you're not telling me you believe in ghosts?"

"I didn't . . . I don't." He seemed at a loss for words. "I don't know, but I know there's something down there in that swamp. I saw it that one time I went down there." He sat back in his chair and took another sip of beer.

"Well, daddy, you gonna tell us, or make us guess?"

"Okay, okay, I'll tell you." He put his beer back on the table. "When we was little, my daddy said to stay away from the swamp, and not to go out at night, but it wasn't because of ghosts, it was 'cause he was scairt we'd end up missin'."

"Why?" I asked.

Rowena snapped her fingers. "Oh yeah, I remember that. Kids from around here and as far away as Lufkin and Nacogdoches were going missing up until about ten years ago. That's why you never let us go out alone at night, or down to the swamp any time?"

I looked from one to the other, pretty sure the confusion I felt was obvious.

"The missing kids is why I wouldn't let you kids go out at night, but the swamp's another matter," Winston said. "I hadn't thought 'bout that night for a long time." He then leaned forward, and in a husky voice not much above a whisper began to tell a story that had the hairs on the back of my neck tingling.

"I was pretty big for my age, even when I was twelve," he said. "But, my daddy was big, too, and that old man didn't take no guff off nobody. You get outta line, and he'd make you cut your own switch to get your butt whupped. Anyway, I guess I was just too stubborn for my own good. Daddy say stay away from the swamp, I just had to go see what it was about. He say don't go out by yourself after dark, I figure I was big enough to take care of myself."

"So, you went down to the swamp?" Rowena asked. "What happened?"

He glared at her. "Hush up, girl, and let me tell my story. Daddy was more worried 'bout me goin' out by myself after dark than he was the swamp. Like I said, it was 'cause kids had been goin' missin' for two or three years. Ever year 'round 'bout July or August, I think, another kid would just up and disappear."

"What do you mean, disappear?" I asked.

"Just what I done said." He looked irritated. "One day they be there, the next day they be gone. Had folks plumb spooked."

I tried to get my head around what he was saying. Seemed to me this would have had to trigger some kind of law enforcement alert.

"What did the authorities do about it?"

"They didn't do shit," Winston said. His eyes blazed. "The kids that went missin' were colored boys, except for one white boy whose folks were poor white sharecroppers from up near Shelbyville, and he only rated a little bit higher than colored. You got to remember, Al, this was back in the fifties and sixties, back then most colored folks 'round here didn't have telephones and only a few had TVs, and the law didn't give a shit what happened to colored folks. Oh, they'd come out and listen to a family complain, but then they'd go back to town and write it off as just another runaway nigger."

"Okay, I can understand that attitude in the 1950s and even the 60s, but Rowena just said this was happening as recently as ten years ago. Surely they took it seriously then?"

"Well, they did send out a few search parties and such, but they ain't never found nothin', so they done wrote 'em off as runaways, and stop lookin'. In the 70s, things was a little better, but not a whole lot. The new sheriff back then, who happens to be the sheriff now, too, he took it more seriously than the ones before, but he couldn't find nothin', so they just quit lookin'."

That, unfortunately, I knew to pretty much be the case countrywide. With between one and three million teens a year running away from home, meager police resources are stretched thin. In poor rural areas it has to be particularly problematic.

I looked at Rowena. "But, you say, it stopped about ten years ago?"

"Yeah, it's kinda strange," she said. "For the longest time, we'd hear about another missing boy every year. Then, since about . . . I don't know, maybe ten, fifteen years ago, we haven't had anybody from around here go missing."

"I wonder why we never heard anything about this up where I lived," I said.

Winston shook his head. "It wasn't something folks liked to talk about. I remember one time we was visiting your folks and I said somethin', and my daddy near 'bout knocked my head off. I guess it never happened up your way."

All I could do was shake my head. Nearly half a century of missing kids, and it apparently didn't even rate a footnote. I did some quick mental calculations. At a kid a year, that came to as many as fifty missing kids, and there'd been no national media coverage, nothing on '60 Minutes,' no documentaries. Runaways are a national problem, but this was a national disgrace.

"Well, I can certainly understand why your father didn't want you going out alone at night."

He nodded, still looking solemn. "Now, though, I got to tell you 'bout the haint." I smiled at his use of the quaint local term for ghost or spirit. "I know this girl of mine think I'm squirrelly in the head, but what I'm 'bout to tell you is the truth."

71

"I never said you were squirrelly, daddy," Rowena protested. "I just didn't know you believe in ghosts."

"You just hush up and listen to my story, and then you tell me if you still think I'm crazy.

He took a sip of beer, and shook himself like a big bear emerging from a creek.

"One night, I snuck out of the house after everybody was sleep. Musta been 'round midnight I reckon. I made my way down to the swamp. I had me one of them coal oil lamps, but I didn't need it. You could find that swamp with your eyes closed 'cause of the smell. I swear, that stank make a pig pen smell like a perfume factory."

"That's for sure," Rowena said. "Sometimes, when the wind's blowing from that direction, you can smell it up here at the house."

Winston glared at her, but said nothing. She shrank back with an innocent smile on her face.

"Anyway, I was goin' down to see what all the fuss was about," he said. "Man, the smell from that place was so strong it made my eyes water, but I was determined to go on. 'Bout ten yards in it though, I saw the lights."

"Lights? You mean like swamp gas?"

"Naw, it wasn't no swamp gas," he said, shaking his head adamantly. "I know what swamp gas look like, and this wasn't it. It was orange, kinda like my coal oil lamp, but it wasn't flickerin' like a lamp. It did move, though, kinda like it was floatin' in the air. I nearly pissed my pants when I saw it. I dropped that coal oil lamp and lit outta there back to the house."

I had to give Winston credit; he told a great story. I remembered how he used to thrill me when I was a kid with his stories. But, the look in his eyes, a kind of haunted look, told me this one wasn't made up.

"Wow," I said. "It can't get much worse than that."

He laughed. "Oh, hell yes it can. I was screamin' so loud when I run back into the yard, I woke my daddy up. He whupped me for disobeying, and then whupped me some more for losing the lamp. That's the last time I went into that swamp."

"Seems to me then you should be glad to get rid of it."

Winston's brow wrinkled, and he sighed deeply. "In a way, I would like to be shed of it," he said. "And, I don't like that asshole Dudley Jarvis pressuring me like he's doin'. But, I just got me a strange feelin' 'bout this Caldwell fella too. I don't think he tellin' me the whole truth, you know. I don't like it when somebody try to cheat me."

I let his words linger in the air. The three of us were silent for a long time, just sitting there listening to the night noises. I don't know what Winston and Rowena were thinking, but my mind was mapping out a plan of attack. First, I had to find out what Loren Caldwell was about. I was pretty sure his story about scientific research was bullshit. It was a land grab, but for what purpose? Jarvis was an entirely different story. I know Winston had said he could handle the man, but my curiosity was aroused. He seemed extremely emotional about the possibility of Winston selling his land. Suspicion of outsiders is hardwired into the genes of East Texans, but his reaction was over the top even by local standards.

I would have to wait and see what Heather could dig up on Caldwell, but the Jarvis farm was right next door to Winston's place. Maybe I needed to pay them a little visit.

"Winston, the Jarvis property is adjacent to yours, right?" I said.

"Yeah, it is, why?"

"I just thought I ought to check out that area. Maybe it'll give me an idea why Jarvis is so hot about you selling. I don't buy that 'we don't want strangers settling here' argument of his."

"Okay, Al, but a good bit of the line between our places is that swamp land, and that whole area's full of snakes, scorpions, and spiders."

I shivered involuntarily. There aren't many things that scare me. I can, for instance, deal with snakes. When I was in the army, I attended the jungle training school that the army ran in Panama, and one of the first classes introduced snakes. If you're going to operate in the jungle, getting beyond the irrational fear of snakes that most of us have is essential. I did okay there. Scorpions and spiders, though, are an entirely different matter. Snakes, except cobras during mating season and copperheads any time, aren't really aggressive. They only attack when frightened or provoked. Scorpions, though, strike anything that gets near them, and getting stung by a scorpion is like being stabbed with a white-hot needle, and if you're allergic, can be fatal. Spiders also spook me. Not because they're aggressive, but because they just look dangerous, and they're everywhere. The kind of spiders you find in jungles and swamps are especially nasty looking.

"Don't worry," I said. "I have no intention of going into the swamp. I just want to see where the two property lines link up."

Rowena snickered. "You're not scared of snakes are you?"

"No, cousin, I'm not afraid of snakes. I do, however, have a healthy respect for them. My motto is, don't go looking for trouble and maybe trouble won't come looking for you."

I knew it sounded like total bull, and the smirk on her face said that she did too.

Then, she threw me a curve, by changing the subject. "You ever think about coming back home, Al?"

"Huh? Oh, you mean come back to Texas?"

"That's your home. Where'd you think I meant?"

Good question. Thomas Wolfe wrote a book, *You Can't Go Home Again.* I remember reading it during one of my deployments when I'd run out of mystery novels, couldn't sleep, and needed something to occupy my waking hours. It took me a long time to really understand what I think he meant, and I'm not sure I got it right. But, what I concluded is that home isn't just a physical place, it's more an emotional anchorage. I couldn't return to Texas, because I no longer had any emotional attachment to the place. No graves to visit, no places occupying a fond place in my heart and memories, no one I was particularly attached to. Before Sara and Ethan died, home for me had been wherever we were, because *they* were my home. For a long time afterwards, I lived in a house, but it never felt like home. And then, Sandra came into my life, and bit by bit, my little farm house off River Road started to feel like a home.

"My home's in Washington now," I said. "Actually, in Maryland, just outside Washington."

Chapter 9

My eyes snapped open at 5:30 the next morning, my normal wake up time.

Despite an overly-large beer and staying on the porch talking with Winston and Rowena until well past 10:00, I woke up feeling refreshed.

I decided to use the walk across Winston's fields to the property line between his place and the Jarvis farm for my exercise rather than my usual morning run, so instead of sweats, I pulled on black cargo pants, a black sweater, and my black canvas jungle boots. I debated wearing the black knit cap, but figured what the hell, it was daytime, at 5:30 it was already starting to feel hot, and I didn't need the sweat in my eyes.

My virtuous feeling was dampened as I exited the back door, when I saw Winston coming out of the dairy barn.

"Hey, Al," he said, waving. "You're up early."

"Yeah, I thought I'd walk over and take a look at your swamp."

"Well, the cool of the morning's a good time to do it, 'cause the snakes won't be active. But, I don't think it's such a good idea."

I wiped at the thin sheen of sweat that had collected on my brow after only a few seconds. If this was the *cool* of the morning, I couldn't wait for *hot*.

"I wasn't planning on actually going into the swamp," I said. "I'm just planning to walk along the edge to get a look."

"Be careful anyway. There's copperheads in the grass near the swamp, and that's one mean snake. Why, the damn things'll come right at you if you get near 'em."

I promised I'd keep a sharp eye out, and jogged off toward the cornfield. The corn was high, and the stalks were heavy with large ears of corn. In a couple of months Winston and his two men would be busy harvesting what looked like a bumper crop. As I walked briskly the long, spiky leaves made rasping noises against my jacket. The tops of the stalks were about a foot above my head, blocking my view of everything but the gray-blue sky.

After twenty minutes of walking, I stepped out of the cornfield into a field of what Winston called his truck crops. Cabbage, lettuce, peas, beans, and carrots, about ten acres of low-lying greenery and neat rows of rich black earth stretched out before me. Beyond that I could see the start of the pasture land which led to the swamp, which was marked by a dark line of trees. The air around me changed. In the corn, it had been still and dust-laden, carrying a slightly sweet odor. Out here among the low-growing crops, the air brushed gently against my face and the rich, musky smell of the rich earth tickled my nostrils. In the pasture, with its knee-high grass, there was an odor that reminded me of a freshly-cut lawn. The breeze had picked up, and the waving grass made a whispering sound. Up closer, I could see that the trees beyond the pasture were a mixture of oak, hickory, and pine, and beyond that the spreading umbrella of cypress. The earth was spongy beneath my boots and had the wet, rotting humus smell I remembered from the many jungles I'd trekked through. Occasionally, the wind would shift, and I'd catch a whiff of the rotten-egg smell of the swamp, strong enough to make my eyes water. Forget the snakes, spiders and scorpions, or even the possibility of the occasional alligator; the specter of ghosts or troubled spirits, if you believed in such things; or even the eerie sights you see in a swamp at night, like the gnarled trunks, tangled roots, and grasping limbs of cypress trees; the smell alone should be enough to keep anyone from wanting to explore this place

I tried to imagine a bunch of geologists, wearing gas masks and rubber suits, stumbling around in a place like this, digging bore holes that would fill with fetid water, and ducking snakes and biting creatures, and I just couldn't get my mind around it. Hell, I was a good hundred yards from the swamp, and already had a cloud of gnats swarming around my head, and the occasional dragonfly dive bombing me. I was also aware of the rising temperature, which raised the possibility of snakes crawling through the high grass in search of food. I angled to my left and made my way toward the three-strand barbed wire fence that separated Winston's farm from the Jarvis place. The grass was only ankle-high for a distance of six feet from the fence, probably kept short to facilitate checking and repairing the fence. The ground near the fence was also drier, making crunching sounds under my boots.

A few meters from the tree line the smell got so strong it began to make my nose drip and my eyes hurt, and the fence stopped. The last pole was no more than ten meters from the nearest stand of trees, the three strands of wire twisted together and hanging downward. I stopped and surveyed the area.

The trees extended a good twenty to thirty yards onto the Jarvis farm, so I assumed that the swamp did as well. Keeping to Winston's side of the fence, but well in the shorter grass, I moved forward, breathing shallow in an effort to ease the stench coming from the trees.

A movement to my left caught my eye. A high bush at the edge of the tree line about twenty yards from me swayed. There wasn't enough wind to do it, and none of the other plants moved. Whatever had caused the movement it had to be pretty big. East Texas has a variety of wildlife, a few deer, the occasional bear, panthers, and, probably most dangerous of all, wild boar. A boar can weigh in at five hundred pounds, and its razor sharp tusks can rip a man to pieces. Worse, while most wildlife will shy away from human contact, these porcine monsters have a personality that's as ugly as their appearance, and they move fast, making them pretty hard to outrun. The best advice I'd ever heard on how to deal with them was, avoid them.

I stopped and stood still, focusing on the bush that had moved. The only sounds were the distant caw of a flock of crows and my slow and steady breathing. We inherited from our ancient ancestors an almost automatic response to unknown situations, or possible threats; the fight or flight response, our brain tells the rest of our body to prepare to either fight or 'get the hell out of Dodge.' Our senses go on hyper-alert as we scan our immediate surroundings for the 'enemy.' Pulse rates quicken, and our muscles prepare to defend or dash. Most people have no control over this. My time in the army had taught me to, though; I let the sensory organs do their thing, as I scanned the area, but instead of my muscles tensing up, I left them relaxed. Oh, I was prepared to fight if there was danger and it was within my capability to handle, or run like the wind if it was a wild boar. But I slowed my breathing to conserve energy and not hyperventilate, which also kept my heart rate within bounds.

The senses were working well. I heard the rustling of something in the bushes, not moving toward me, not moving at all, but more like something squirming around. I took a deep breath and exhaled slowly. It wasn't a boar. Had it been, it probably would've been charging at me already.

"Hello," I said. "Who's there?"

The rustling sound stopped.

"Come on out, whoever you are?"

The bush began to quiver. Then, I realized that behind that bush was the deadliest animal of all. Dudley Jarvis stood up. He had a double barrel shotgun held over his right shoulder and glared at me. He stepped from behind the bush and approached me, stopping about six feet away. The smell of rotten eggs or something worse wafted off his body, and he left a muddy trail from the bush. He'd been walking through the swamp.

"What you doin' out here," he said. "You ain't got no business snoopin' 'round our farm."

I looked around. I pointed to the fence. "The way I see it, it's not me that's doing the snooping. I'm standing on Winston Jones's property, and your left foot's crossed the property line. What are *you* doing snooping around my cousin's farm?"

He looked down at the offending foot and up at the fence line, then took two steps to his right. He at least had the decency to look embarrassed. "Oh, sorry, my mistake," he said. "I didn't see the fence. Thought I was still on our land."

"No problem. I'm pretty sure my cousin doesn't mind." I pointed at the shotgun. "You out hunting today?"

His hand tightened on the stock of the weapon. "Uh . . . yeah . . . that's what I was doin'. Thought I might shoot a rabbit for the pot tonight." His eyelids did a little dance as he spoke, and he looked at a point on the ground about three feet in front of me.

I decided to ignore his lie. No one in his right mind hunted rabbits with a shotgun, unless they wanted to eat shredded meat. I wanted to get some information from him, so no point alienating him, I thought.

"Say, you mind if I ask a personal question?"

He looked at me through narrow slits and his brow wrinkled. "What kind of question?"

"Did you get an offer to buy any of your land?"

A flicker of annoyance crossed his face.

"Naw, we didn't," he said. "Why you want to know?"

"Just curious. Part of the swamp's on your land, right?"

"Yeah, a little bit of it is on our side of the line, but most of it's on Winston's land."

"But, you'd think they'd want to buy the whole shebang, right?"

He blinked. I could almost hear him thinking, wondering what I was getting at.

"I reckon. Ain't got no idea why they'd want any of it. Ain't nothin' in there but snakes and gators. You don't want to go in there, it's got quicksand, too. You fall in one of them quicksand holes, your body'd never be found."

"I suppose it wouldn't be smart to go in there at night," I said.

He glared at me. "It ain't smart to go in there *no* time, night or day. Gators and snakes ain't got watches, and they'll take a bite out your ass any time."

That was true, but I didn't think he really gave a rat's ass about my safety. I'm no fan of alligators or snakes, am not fond of wading through shitty-smelling water, but he seemed just too anxious to keep me out of that swamp.

So, of course, that meant that sooner or later I'd have to explore it.

First, though, I needed to ping Heather and see if she'd learned anything about Caldwell and his desire to buy a worthless piece of land.

"Well," I said. "I guess I'll get on back to the house. I have no desire to go up against snakes *or* gators."

"That sounds like a right smart idea to me," he said.

He stood there, a few feet onto his own property, the shotgun still over his shoulder, watching as I walked away.

Chapter 10

Even though I'd walked, and at a leisurely pace at that, by the time I got back to the house, I was soaking wet. It was only 10:00 am, but the temperature was in the high eighties, and the humidity was at ninety percent; the kind of weather that sucks the energy out of every pore along with the sweat.

There was no one in the kitchen when I entered through the back door, so I dashed through and took the stairs two at a time heading up to the second floor. I was peeling off my clothes before I made it to the bathroom, and by the time I pulled the door open was down to my skivvies.

A high-pitched squeal brought me up short in my shorts.

Rowena stood at the sink, one towel wrapped around her head, and another wrapped around her body, barely containing her breasts, and not coming together at the back because of her ample measurements in that area. When the door opened, she whirled around and squealed, but not before I got two eyes full of the globes or her butt where the towel didn't come together, and noticed that her thighs, though shapely, came together from knee upwards instead of having that little gap between them that a lot of women have.

I jumped back into the hallway and slammed the door shut.

"I'm sorry, Rowena," I said. "I didn't know you were in there." I grabbed my pants from the floor and pulled them on.

"That's okay; you just startled me is all." Her voice was muffled through the door. "You need to take a shower?"

"Uh, yeah, but I can wait, you go ahead and finish up." I grabbed my shirt, socks, and boots and beat a hasty retreat to my room.

My boots and sweaty socks were in a jumble at the foot of the bed, and I sat on the edge in pants and shirt, sniffing at my underarm—and, not enjoying the experience—when there was a soft knock on the door.

"Al," Rowena said. "You okay in there?"

"Of course I am," I said. "Why shouldn't I be?"

I heard her chuckle. "Aw, come on, I saw the tent pole in your shorts. You liked what you saw, didn't you?"

"Rowena, you're interpreting an involuntary physical reaction for something entirely different." That involuntary reaction had long since receded. "Trust me, there's no way in hell it would go any further than that."

"Why not?" There was a tremor in her voice. "You think I'm ugly or something?"

I did not like the direction this conversation was taking.

"Not at all, Rowena," I said. "I think you're a fine looking woman."

"So, why are you hiding from me?"

Damnit, it was time to nip this thing in the bud.

"I'm not hiding. I'm just waiting for you to finish up in the bathroom and get dressed so I can take a shower."

"I'm done," she said. "So, you can come out and take your shower. You don't have to hide from me, you know. You don't have anything I haven't already seen, although, I have a feeling yours looks better."

"Cut it out, Rowena. We're relatives, and this is completely inappropriate."

"Aw, we're cousins, and probably third or fourth cousins at that. We wouldn't be breaking any laws done here. Hell, I know cousins that are married to each other."

"We might not be breaking any laws, but we'd damn sure be doing something wrong. Besides, I'm old enough to be your father."

"I like older men."

"I'm in a relationship."

"We don't have to tell her, and what she doesn't know won't hurt anyone."

This was getting ridiculous. The woman was as stubborn as a mule, which didn't surprise me. My family is known for being hardheaded. Then, I remember another thing my family is known for. "Rowena, if you don't stop this nonsense, I'm gonna tell Winston what you're up to. Bet he'd still tan your backside."

There was a long moment of silence. Then, the sound of bare feet scuffing the floor boards. "Shoot, you're no fun at all. I guess I'll have to go into town to find me some action." I waited near the door until the slap of her feet against the floor faded.

I opened the door and peeked out. The hallway was empty. I knew the threat of telling Winston would work, but I'd kept my fingers crossed. My family is known for stern discipline. You do not cross the head of the family, no matter your age.

She was cute, but there was no way I was going down that road. I remembered a couple of my cousins who were visiting when I was about eight. We'd gone to my grandmother's house, and they'd left me in the living room reading some of the books on the shelves in the corner. My grandmother caught them in a closet playing doctor. After a stern talking to, where they were told they would burn in hell for what they did, she took them one at a time to the tool shed. Even from the back porch, thirty feet away, I could hear the 'whap' of the leather strap she used on them, and their screams of pain. As far as she was concerned, cousins were blood, and no matter how thin that connection might be, they were off limits to each other. Obviously, Rowena's grandmother had a different set of standards, or she'd never been caught, but I wasn't about to become a kissing cousin.

I grabbed some clean clothes and scooted to the bathroom. After I'd showered and changed, I went back to my room and retrieved my phone. It was time to get to work. I called Heather.

"Hey, boss man, you must be psychic. I was about to call you. I wanted to catch you before I take off for lunch."

In all the years we've worked together, I've never known Heather to go out for lunch. She usually has a salad she brings from home and eats at her desk.

"Going out? Is there something I need to know?"

"Uh, not really," she said. "I, uh, met this guy when I was at Safeway the other day, and he invited me to lunch, okay."

"No problem, just asking. I assume you were gonna call me for the same reason I'm calling you, an update on this guy Caldwell?"

"Yeah." I sensed from her tone that she was happy to direct the conversation away from her lunch date. "I'm still digging, but, I can tell you one thing; there's no such outfit as GeoSync unless it's some kind of government black bag operation."

I stifled the impulse to ask if she was sure. When it comes to ferreting out information on people or organizations, Heather could teach the CIA a few things. If it exists, especially in our computer age, there's a record of it somewhere, and if there's a record anywhere but the sealed vaults of NSA or CIA, Heather will find it.

"So, you're saying that this guy Caldwell might be some kind of deep cover government operative? What the hell would the government want with a useless piece of swamp land in East Texas?"

"Al, you really need to get the cotton out of your ears. I never said anything about Caldwell. I said that GeoSync does not exist, at least, not as a legitimate research organization."

"Okay, I got that part, but Caldwell's claiming that he works for GeoSync, so—"

"Anyone can claim to work for any organization," she said, and rather testily at that. "For about ten bucks you can get name cards printed up at a dozen shops here in DC. I imagine you can do the same down there in cow country."

"You care to explain that, or do I have to guess?"

"Whether Loren Caldwell works for GeoSync or not depends on whether or not it exists . . . and my money says it doesn't exist. What I do know, though, is that a Loren Caldwell is vice president for acquisitions and development for Global Energy of Lufkin, Texas."

"What is Global Energy?"

"It's a second-rate energy company," she said. "They deal in oil, coal, and natural gas. I'm still digging, but there are ticklers that say they've been involved in some shady deals in the past."

"Shady deals like cheating landowners?"

"I don't know yet what kind of shady deals. I've just read a couple of reports that said they were investigated, but no charges have ever been filed, and there are no court cases. I'm still working on the details."

The details were important, but if Caldwell was lying about who he really worked for, and he was willing to offer Winston a hundred grand for his land, it was a good bet in my book that the land was worth a hell of a lot more. Mr. Caldwell and I were going to have another little talk, only this time, I planned to get the truth out of him even if I had to squeeze a little in order to do it.

"Get back to me as soon as you have 'em, Heather," I said. "I guess I'll have to drop in on Mr. Caldwell this afternoon."

"I'll do that." I could hear the sound of paper rustling and desk drawers being slammed shut. "Oh, one other thing before I let you go; I ran a check on Dudley Jarvis, your cousin's neighbor. No criminal record, and no indication that he's ever belonged to the Klan or anything like that."

I laughed. "Except for being a bit pushy, he seems to get along with Winston," I said. "I'm just curious as to why the idea of Winston selling any of his land bothers him so."

"You got me there, boss man. All I've been able to find out so far is that he grew up there in Poseyville, enrolled in Baylor University in 1971, but dropped out and came back home after only two years. He's an only child whose mother died the year he dropped out of school, so now he lives on the family place with his father, Henry Jarvis. The elder Jarvis is an invalid according to one record I found, but it didn't say what his illness is. That help?"

I wanted to say that it didn't help, but she'd gone out of her way to get it. "Yeah, a little," I said. "Let me know if you come up with anything else. Say, wait a minute, you say Jarvis enrolled in college in 1971? That would make his age early fifties, right?"

"Yeah, he was born in 1953, why?"

"Oh, it's just that he looks so much older. I would have pegged him at my age or even older. I guess working on a farm ages you."

"I wouldn't know," she said. "Now, can I go to lunch? My ride's here."

"Sure, Honeybunch," I said, using the pet name that I gave her when she came to work for me right out of secretarial school, before the age of political correctness when such an appellation given to a female employee would get you hauled into the human resources office for counseling, and which she allowed no one else but me to use. "Sorry if I held you up. You have a good lunch, and I'll talk to you later."

"Okay, bye," she said. From the way 'bye' faded, I knew she was hanging up as she spoke.

I chuckled as I stuffed my phone into my shirt pocket. Good for her, I thought. Heather hadn't had a love interest the whole time I'd known her, hadn't really shown any interest in men. I was beginning to worry that she'd never find anyone. Since Sandra and I made our exclusive relationship 'official,' I'd begun realizing that being alone didn't have much to recommend itself. I'd almost become like the worrisome aunt who's always trying to fix you up with her neighbor's daughter or her hair dresser's sister. I hadn't actually tried matching her up with anyone, but it was on my mind a lot. Thinking of Heather with a date, made me think of Sandra and how much I missed her.

But, I had things to do. I mentally put the Jarvis family on the back burner. I was still curios about their concern over the sale, but priority had to go to shining some light on Caldwell's dark intentions. That meant pulling information out of Caldwell, but it also meant visiting the swamp to see what all the fuss was about. That latter task, thanks to the probability that Jarvis was keeping an eye on it, dictated that I pay a nocturnal visit, not exactly something I was looking forward to, and certainly not until I'd picked up a few essential supplies.

Chapter 11

I found Winston in one of the big chicken sheds. The long, low building, little more actually than steel pilings set in concrete to which corrugated iron panels were attached to serve as walls and roof, each housed ten thousand squawking, crapping chickens. The floor was packed dirt, over which a two inch layer of sawdust had been poured. The constant movement of the chickens, or of anyone entering the structure, created a cloud of sawdust that hung in the air. During the day, the birds were constantly moving and squabbling over food which was available in long metal troughs set in the long walls. The troughs were constantly replenished with the grain the chickens ate from a large box-like structure mounted on the wall at the front. The feed poured down through metal conduits into the troughs and was moved along by a conveyer belt, a lattice-like contraption of wood and plastic, in the bottom of each. I got a brief glimpse of the interior as Winston exited. One whiff of the air, with the tickling sensation of sawdust, and the musty odor of chicken manure, and the assault upon my ears from ten thousand birds that only become quiet at night, was enough to dissuade me from entering.

Winston was covered from head to foot in a fine patina of gray dust, and his body and clothing exuded a milder version of what I'd smelled through the open door. When he slapped at the bib of his overalls, puffs of dust billowed, and more of that odor d'chicken shed wafted my way.

I wrinkled my nose.

"Hey," he said. "It ain't as bad as it used to be when we had to do everything by hand. Imagine what it was like, shoveling a ton of chicken shit out of that sawdust every day."

"Thanks, but I'd rather not."

"Of course, it can still be messy. You ought to be around when we get ready to send 'em off to market."

"What's so messy about that?"

"That's a part we still do by hand. Juan and Diego hire a buncha their friends and we go in 'bout midnight and remove 'em by hand."

"Why so late?"

"That's when they sleep," he said. "And, it's easier to grab 'em by the leg and hoist 'em into the shippin' crates. It takes 'bout four hours for six men to clear out a shed, and at the end of it, they're covered in chicken shit and sawdust."

"Remind me not to be around when that happens. Say, I need to buy some hunting and fishing gear, and a couple of flashlights. Where's the nearest place I can do that?"

"Hardware store downtown's got most everything you might need," he said. "You ain't still plannin' to go into that swamp? And, at night? That's puree-dee crazy."

"I can[t argue the point, but a man's gotta do what a man's gotta do."

Despite being unable to dissuade me from visiting the swamp, he did convince me to wait until after lunch to do my shopping, which, as soon as we entered the kitchen, I regretted. Rowena had been assigned lunch duty, and she was in the kitchen when we entered. She smiled at me and cocked her left eyebrow as I passed her, and kept sneaking little glances at me throughout lunch. I ate fast. Another mistake.

* * *

My stomach grumbled all the way into town, so my first stop was a drugstore— fortunately only two shops down from the hardware store—where I bought a package of Tums. I opened it and began chewing two before I even left the store.

By the time I got to the hardware store, the grumbling had subsided, so that at least I was able to do what I came to do in relative peace and quiet. My stomach had been rumbling so loud, I was worried I'd be cited for violating some noise ordinance.

Winston had been right about Poseyville's hardware store being a one-stop shop for anything to do with hunting, fishing, or building. The place was huge inside, and had everything from band saws to four-man tents to shotguns. It was not only a hardware store, but a sporting goods and gun shop. Only in Texas.

There were four people, who didn't appear to be customers; a fat man, with a large, bald head, in a denim jacket who sat on a stool behind the main counter near the cash register watching everyone. I took him to be the owner. I spotted four customers, all older men dressed in the local farmers' preferred outfit, overalls and denim shirts. There were three young guys who stood around looking bored until someone asked them for help, at which time, they moved with surprising speed to lift boxes, or demonstrate tools. They all looked alike, and except for the lack of hair, like the fat man. Like a lot of small town shops, it was a family business.

One of the young men, who looked to be in his mid-twenties, intercepted me as I headed toward a display of knives and rifles at the back of the store.

"Can I help you, sir?" he asked in a high pitched voice.

I pointed at the knives. "Do you happen to have K-Bar knives in that display?" I'd left my trusty K-Bar at home in my closet. I could've put it in my checked baggage, but only two years after 9/11, the TSA munchkins at Dulles Airport were still acting like the Gestapo, and I didn't want to have my duffel, which was a bit too big to fit in the overhead bin on my flight, torn apart if the x-ray machine they used on checked baggage detected a knife.

"Yup, we sure do." He squeezed past me and nearly sprinted to the display case.

By the time I arrived, he'd already taken a knife from the shelf and was holding it up for my inspection. I took it and hefted it. The K-Bar, trademarked as KA-BAR, was first adopted as a fighting knife by the Marine Corps in 1942, and with its 7-inch carbon steel blade and leather washer handle is the best knife in the world for close-in combat or utility cutting if you're in the field.

"How much for this one?" I asked.

"With the leather sheath, and that's real leather, by the way, that'll come to seventy dollars."

He squinted at me, as if expecting me to argue over the price. A brand new knife like this one would go for up to ninety bucks back east, so it was a bargain.

"I'll take it," I said. "I also need a few more items, so just put that on the counter until I'm done shopping . . . or should I get a cart and just pile everything in?"

He looked disappointed at first, then a broad smile lit up his freckled face.

"Whyn't you jest take a cart," he said, pointing to a row of nested shopping carts at the end of the counter. "Jest bring everything to the front counter when you're done."

I thanked him and took the knife, slipped it into the black leather sheath and walked over to the carts. I pulled the rear cart out and placed the knife gently in the bottom. The kid was still standing behind the counter looking like he'd just opened the box containing a new American Flyer bike at Christmas.

"Where would I find waders?" I asked.

He pointed to the far corner. "You need 'em for fishin' or duck huntin'?"

"What's the difference?"

"Well, the waders for huntin' got sturdier boots, more pockets for carryin' ammo and such, and they come in camouflage colors."

"Like for hunting at night?"

"Yep, black and green's perfect for night huntin', 'cept you ain't gon' be shootin' no ducks at night."

"No, but I am gonna be hunting swamp creatures, and I've heard that's best done at night."

He looked around quickly, then came from behind the counter and rushed over to me. "Say, mister," he said in a voice just above a whisper. "You shouldn't be sayin' that too loud 'round here.

My breath caught in my throat. Could someone other than Jarvis and Caldwell know about the land deal?

"I mean, we do a little gator huntin' ourselves, me, pa and my brothers, I mean. It's near 'bout the end of the season, and it won't start up again until September. And, another thing, if you gonna shoot 'em, don't git caught doin' it on public land."

I let my breath out.

"Damn, sorry, I wasn't thinking." Thank goodness for the fraternity of diehard hunters. The kid thought I was a poacher, and he was happy to conspire with me, as long as I didn't broadcast it too loudly.

"You're gonna need a good flashlight, too," he said. "We can also make you a good deal on a rifle and some ammo."

The flashlight sounded like a good idea, but I gave guns up before I left the army. A mission that went south resulting in the unfortunate deaths of several noncombatants soured me on firearms. Since that mission, I'd only used a gun once, and that was to take out a rogue FBI agent who was about to put a hole in me. Even though it was justified, I felt bad about it for almost a year. Heather and I do our annual firearms qualification shooting at the Montgomery County police shooting range as a requirement for our PI licenses, but neither of us owns or carries a piece. I figure if I'm unable to fight my way out of a situation with hands or feet—I have black belts in three forms of Oriental martial arts—I can always run away.

"I can use my cousin's rifle," I said, which was true had that been my intent, because I was pretty sure Winston, like every other Texan, had one. "I just need some personal gear."

"Well, like I said. You're gonna need a good flashlight."

"Why don't you show me what you think I need—minus the rifle, that is."

He was more than happy to guide me, quietly discussing the best places in the county to find the gnarly creatures, and all the ways there were to bag them—shooting (not recommended because of legal limitations), bow and arrow, hook and line, and gigging. The latter sounded interesting, albeit pretty damned dangerous. Using what looked like a giant's fork, you sneak up on the alligator and stab it like taking frogs. Of course, if you miss a frog, it hops away. Miss a gator and he just might make you sorry you disturbed him. I had no intention of trying to kill an alligator by any method, but the alligator gig looked like a handy weapon, so I threw one into the cart. By the time we'd finished, I had the knife, a pair of black and green chest waders, a regular LED tactical flashlight, an infrared tactical flashlight, and a frog gig. The infrared light was for making my way through the dark swamp and spotting animals without startling them, and the regular light to temporarily blind them before stabbing them with the gig. With the ten percent Texas sales tax, the bill came to five hundred dollars. The bald guy frowned when I whipped out my credit card to pay, but when he saw it was issued by the United Services Automobile Association, he smiled and began to ring it up. USAA is an insurance and banking association that was founded in 1922 when a bunch of army officers got together and decided to insure each other's cars. My card marked me as either active duty or veteran, and in Texas either status counts.

The old man beamed at me as the light on his phone blinked green to show that my card was good for the amount of purchase, thanked me for my service, and had the kid who'd helped me shop carry my purchases to my car for me.

With my purchases secured in the cargo compartment of the 4-Runner, I drove to Caldwell's motel for a 'come to Jesus' meeting with him.

* * *

I parked at the entrance nearest the conference center next to a silver BMW that looked from the outside like it had all the options. Hardly a car one would expect to see in a small farming town like Poseyville. Fortunately, the 'Room Card Key Required' lock was disabled allowing me to enter. Caldwell's rented digs were near the entry, which explained the ability to enter without a key. He'd no doubt paid hotel staff to disable the lock to allow him and his 'customers' easy access.

When I entered the reception area, the same woman was sitting at the same desk, but Caldwell was standing over her staring down the front of her dress where an ample amount of her cleavage was on display. She had a bemused expression on her face as she flipped idly through a copy of *People* magazine, while he, with his red cheeks and slightly bulging eyes, looked like he was about to have a heart attack.

I cleared my throat. He looked up, his eyes went even wider, and he jumped back a few inches, looking like a kid who just got caught with his hand up a classmate's skirt. His receptionist smiled and kept flipping through the magazine. He moved his hands to quickly cover the bulge in the front of his pants.

"Uh, er, Mr. . . . Pennyback, right? You're back rather quickly. Did you talk your . . . cousin into agreeing to my offer?"

The way the words tumbled out almost made me laugh. But, I didn't come for amusement.

"We need to talk in private, Mr. Caldwell," I said.

His eyes darted from me to the deep valley and rounded mounds showing in the flaring 'v' shape at the front of her blouse and back. The possibility that I represented money won out and they came back and settled on me.

"Yeah, of course." He stepped over and opened the door to the cavernous space that was his office. "Come on in."

As I passed the woman to follow him into his office, she looked up at me with a resigned expression on her face and shrugged.

Inside the office he'd settled himself behind the big desk before I had even crossed the floor. I sat in one of the visitor's chairs and looked across the desk at him.

After several seconds of silence, during which he began to look uncomfortable, he did what I knew he'd do; he broke the silence. "Well, what is it you want to talk to me about?"

"I want you to explain again why you're willing to pay my cousin a hundred thousand dollars for ten worthless acres of land," I said.

He looked at me, his eyes wide. Then, he blinked. "It's just as I told you before," he said. "There could be information underground that would tell us a lot about the ancient past of this region. You can't put a price on knowledge."

The guy was good. He sat there and spun me a completely fabricated yarn with a straight face—too straight. It sounded like a spiel he'd practiced for a long time. How many other suckers had he fed that line?

"Bullshit. Everything has a price. You say you're a research organization; well where does a research organization get the kind of money you're tossing around?"

He blinked again. "Uh, well . . . we have many wealthy donors who are interested in science for science sake."

"Oh yeah, name one."

"I don't think it would be appropriate to do that," he said. "Our donors value their privacy."

"You know, Caldwell, I always thought that Texans were the best when it came to bull crap . . . but, you're really not very good at it you know."

His cheeks flamed red again and he glared at me.

"How dare you! You can't come into my office and insult me like this."

I leaned forward and stabbed a finger at him, stopping it about a foot from his face. He scooted back in his chair, his eyes widened.

"I'm not insulting you, Caldwell," I said. "I'm just stating fact. You're lying through your pearly whites, and I want to know why."

"I, I t-told you, I'm a representative of GeoSync, and we want Win-, Mr. Jones's property to explore the flora and fauna of the Cretaceous Period."

"And, his swamp land is the *only* place to dig for them? I mean, this inland sea you talk about was pretty big. Seems to me if there are bones or whatever under the swamp, they'd be under the dry land next to the swamp. Now, doesn't that make more sense?"

His mouth opened and closed like a fish that's just been taken off a hook and tossed into a creel, as if he was gulping for air. His eyes bounced from one side to the other. He was gulping all right, but not for air, for a way to answer me.

"We, we have our reasons. That's all you need to know."

It wasn't a good answer. It wasn't even a
so-so answer. But a look of determination
was on his face. Short of putting bamboo
slivers under his fingernails, or
waterboarding him, I wasn't getting anything
else from him. I was pretty sure, though, that
Heather would come through with some little
nugget of information I could use to flip him.

"Okay for now, Caldwell," I said. "But, I'm
keeping an eye on you."

I stood and left him sitting there with his
mouth agape.

As I walked through the reception area,
the woman behind the desk put her magazine
down and looked up at me. I stopped and
returned her gaze. She opened her mouth,
and then snapped it shut. There was a
strange look in her eyes, I couldn't pin it
down.

"Are you from around here?" I asked. It
was a lame question, but I had a gut feeling
that she wanted to say something, and it was
the only thing I could think of.

"Yeah, born and bred right here in
Poseyville," she said.

"Have you worked for Mr. Caldwell long?"

"No, just since he came to town." She
looked at the door to his office. "He
advertised for someone to greet visitors and
answer the phone, and I was between jobs.
The manager here is a cousin. He
recommended me."

"You must be quite busy."

She smiled wanly. "Hardly. You're the first
visitor since I started working."

"Lots of phone calls though, right?"

Her brows shot up. "Nope, no phone calls
either. Mr. Caldwell has a direct line on his

desk, and he makes his own calls. He gets two or three calls a day, but they go to his direct line as well." She shrugged. "I just sit here and read my magazines. But, I'm not complaining. I get paid five hundred dollars a week to sit here for eight hours a day. It pays the rent."

"I should be so lucky," I said.

"Yeah, well, you have a nice day." After looking at me with that strange expression for about ten seconds, she sighed and picked up her magazine and began leafing idly through it.

She wanted to tell me something. I knew it. But, this wasn't the time or place to press the issue. Another item on my to-do list. One thing for sure; Caldwell was up to something, and that something wasn't buying land for scientific research.

"Same back at you," I said, and left.

Chapter 12

There always seems to come a time when I'm working a case that I have to pull back and take stock. And, there wasn't a doubt in my mind that this was a case, maybe two cases. On the one hand, I needed to find out what Loren Caldwell was up to, while Dudley Jarvis's interest in my cousin's land was still a puzzle.

In fact, I had two puzzles; the true nature of Caldwell's game, and Jarvis's interest. I'm a sucker for puzzles. Like a person who can never *not* answer a ringing phone, I'm unable to resist an unsolved puzzle.

Caldwell was my number-one priority. My gut was telling me that he was pulling some kind of scam, but for the life of me I couldn't quite figure it out. I was willing to bet, though, that if Heather's information was right, and he worked for an energy company, there was a ton of money involved, and he was maneuvering to cheat Winston out of a fair cut of that money. Sure, a hundred thousand bucks is a lot of money, but if

Caldwell was willing to part with that much, there had to be a hell of a lot more to be had.

There didn't seem to be much hope of getting anything out of him, short of kidnapping him and using coercion on him, and even that gave no guarantees, because, people under physical or mental pressure will tell you whatever they think you *want* to here; trouble it it's seldom what you *need* to hear. I was pretty sure Heather would come up with more information, maybe something I could use as leverage to get him to talk, so I had that card still to play. As I thought about it, I also considered driving to Lufkin, looking up this Global Energy, and see what I might be able to pry out of them.

Then, there was the receptionist. She wanted to tell me something, I was sure of that. Maybe if I got her alone—how I'd go about doing that in a small town where everyone knew everyone else's business was a problem I hadn't quite figured out, another puzzle if you will—I could get her to talk.

Dudley Jarvis was a lesser priority, but I couldn't get his interest in the situation out of my mind. There was more to it than just an aversion to having a stranger as a neighbor. I couldn't put my finger on it, but there was something off about the man. If Heather couldn't find anything more on him, I was just going to have to do a little recce of my own. Maybe drop in to borrow a cup of sugar or a back hoe. Or, maybe just sneak in under cover of darkness and spy on the guy.

I had a third issue. It too was a puzzle, but not a case in and of itself. That damn swamp. Ten acres of boggy land, fetid water, and assorted creatures you don't want to encounter in the dark, it was the thread that tied everyone together. Caldwell wanted to buy it, Jarvis seemed to like walking through it, and, even though he was too scared of it to visit, Winston seemed reluctant to part with it. I was going to have to visit the swamp despite not really wanting to. Well, that's why I bought all that expensive gear.

By the time I parked at the right edge of Winston's front porch, I had a rough plan of operation in mind.

- Check on Caldwell and Global Energy.
- Talk to the receptionist in Poseyville
- Visit Global Energy in Lufkin
- Another talk with Caldwell
- Find out what's up with Jarvis
- Inspect the swamp

Not a short list of things to do at all. I had my work cut out for me.

Under the Jarvis part of the operation, I hadn't come up with any specific steps, but I had a feeling inspecting the swamp might give me some answers to what put the bugs in his britches.

I walked into the living room and headed for the stairs. Rowena came in from the kitchen. She wore a Dallas Cowboys' tee shirt and a white apron over cutoff jeans. Tee shirt and jeans put a generous amount of her flesh on display, and when she walked, I could hear the swish of the denim where her thighs came together.

"You're back from town, I see," she said.

She might be a college student, but she still had the East Texas habit of stating the obvious.

"Yeah," I said.

"You talk to Mr. Caldwell?"

"I did."

"Is he still just offering a hundred thousand?"

"You seem to know a lot about this situation," I said.

"Daddy and I talked about it, we talk about everything" she said. "Well, did Mr. Caldwell raise his offer?"

"We didn't talk about that. I tried to get him to be honest about why he's buying the land in the first place."

She frowned at me, her brow wrinkling. "What difference does it make why he wants to buy it? That's a lot of money he's offering, and heaven knows daddy could use it."

"Really? I thought the farm was doing okay?"

"Oh, it's not doing bad," she said. "But, farming is a risky business. One bad crop, or a spell of bad weather, and you can be wiped out. Daddy's not getting any younger, and he needs to have something put aside for when he retires."

"But, I got the feeling he doesn't want to sell."

She snorted, her nostrils flaring. "Aw, that's just old time sentiment. People around here have this notion somehow that they ought to keep family lands in one piece, even if a piece is worthless. As far as farming's concerned, that swamp land is about as useful as tits on a boar hog. If it's of value to science, why not take advantage of it."

She was making sense, of course. But, I couldn't rid my mind of the nagging feeling that something was rotten about the whole deal. I didn't feel like arguing with her, though.

"I'll talk to him again," I said.

Her brow smoothed out, and the smile returned. She turned and went back to the kitchen. "We'll be having supper early tonight," she said over her shoulder. I went up to my room.

I was sitting on the edge of the bed contemplating my next move when my phone rang. I checked the caller ID before answering, and recognized my office number.

"Hey, honeybunch," I said. "What you got for me?"

"I'm doing fine, and how are you?" The sarcasm in her voice brought me up short. I wondered if her lunch date had been a bust, but decided against asking.

"Sorry, Heather. I just got back from a totally wasted trip into town, and I was preoccupied. How are things going?"

She laughed. "Gotcha. Things are going fine, I just like yanking your chain now and then. Now, sit down and open that big brain of yours and listen, because I have a ton of information to pass along."

I looked around for a pencil or notebook. Nothing, and wouldn't you know it, I'd forgotten to pack notebooks.

"Okay, I'm sitting down," I said. "So shoot."

"First, I haven't found anything else on Loren Caldwell, but since that's not exactly a common name, I think it's safe to assume that the Loren Caldwell listed as employed by Global Energy is your man."

"I'd pretty much come to that same conclusion, but keep digging. There has to be something on him somewhere."

"I can't find any criminal records, and a search of news media in the south and southwest for the past ten years turns up bupkis. It's like the guy doesn't exist except as a name and title on a company website."

That made no sense. If the guy was a senior executive for an energy company, he had to be involved in something that made the paper or local broadcasts. Unless, that is, he didn't normally work in Texas.

"It's an energy company, so they have to have overseas connections. Check reports in areas that are involved in the energy market, you know, the Middle East, Africa. I'll bet this guy will turn up in one of those places."

"Darn, I should have thought of that," she said. "I'll get right on it. Now, Global Energy is another kettle of fish. If they *are* the ones behind the move to buy your cousin's land, you better tell him to count all his fingers after he shakes hands with any of them."

"That's probably true of any of the energy companies, but I have a feeling Global Energy is a special case, right?"

"O-o-oh yes," she said. "They're special all right. The company was founded in November 1973, a month after the Arab oil embargo. Initially, they focused on buying U.S. oil fields and increasing productions. With the spike in oil prices and the shortages caused by the embargo they made a fortune. When the oil started flowing again, they branched out into natural gas, again focusing on domestic sources. The company's stock was trading well until 2001. In the early 1990s they expanded their operations abroad, but the 9/11 attacks disrupted their supplies, and by mid-2002, their stock had started dropping. Since then, they've gone back to mainly domestic production, but they're finding it hard to compete with the big oil companies who are also focusing on domestic sourcing, so they've carved a niche for themselves . . . they look for undeveloped deposits of oil or natural gas on private property and work deals directly with the property owners."

"Don't all the oil and gas companies do that to a certain extent?"

"Yeah, most do, but they also go for public lands. Global is the only one that focuses strictly on private lands, and there are rumors that they're not above using hardball tactics, or deceiving landowners about the value of the property and paying far less than a piece of land is worth."

That thought had been running through my mind.

"Any information about them pretending to be something other than an energy company to acquire land?"

"No, but I wouldn't put it past them. I've just hit the tip of the ice berg on these guys. I'll let you know when I have anything else."

I let out a breath. "Damn, that's a lot to process. Thanks, kid, you've given me a few more cards to play when I speak to Caldwell again. Say, did you get anything else about Jarvis."

"Not Dudley Jarvis." I heard the rustle of paper. "I did pick up some more information on the father, though, Henry Jarvis. He's apparently had a stroke about ten years ago, and is suffering dementia, maybe early onset of Alzheimer's."

That might explain Dudley's feelings about having strangers in the area. Another thing I'd have to look into.

"Thanks," I said. "Looks like I'm gonna be busy the next few days."

"Yeah, me too." She didn't elaborate. I didn't ask. "Oh, one other thing. It hasn't anything to do with your cousin or his land, but when I was researching local media for that area, I found that it has a colorful and bloody history."

"Hell, that could be said for the whole damn state. This is Texas after all."

"I don't mean the usual shoot 'em up stuff. It seems that that area of East Texas, mainly Coquilla and Angelina Counties, between 1951 and 1975 there were a number of missing kids, mostly young black males. They just disappeared and were never found."

"Yeah, my cousin was telling me something about that. The authorities think the kids might have just run away, which makes sense. There's only two kinds of people down here; the ones who never leave, and the ones who leave the first chance they get and never come back. Since this was way back before computers and the internet, it wouldn't have been too hard for someone to disappear. I grew up here and never knew about it. I didn't know it was in the national media."

"Oh," she said in a small voice. "I guess you would know. I just wouldn't ever have associated something like that with a rural area, you know. That's the kind of thing that happens in big cities. Anyway, it wasn't in the national media. I found it in a PhD thesis paper written by some guy at the University of Texas in Austin in 1992, called 'Social Pathology of Rural Texas Counties – Coquilla County's Missing Children.' It came up when I was doing the search on land prices in the area. I read it out of curiosity, and let me tell you, it gave me the creeps."

"Heather, things happen in places like this that make a lot of our big cities look like safe zones. The crap out here in the hinterlands often gets overlooked because it's spread out so much. Did you know, for instance, that East Texas is one of the main transit routes for drugs coming up from Mexico, and some of the small towns here have more meth labs per capita than any big city."

"Criminy, I never thought I'd say I'm glad I live in a city. Okay, just take care of yourself. If these Global Energy folks *are* up to no good, I wouldn't want you disappearing in a swamp or something."

With that cheery thought in mind, I hit the 'end call' button. Little did she know that my encountering trouble in a swamp was a distinct possibility, but a possibility that I felt ready to deal with.

Charles Ray

Chapter 13

During supper, I informed Winston and Rowena of my plans to explore the swamp that night.

Rowena's mouth gaped open so wide that sitting across from her, I could see her uvula. Winston put his fork down and glared at me from his seat at the head of the table.

"Al, you out of your mind? You can't be goin' down in that swamp in the dark," he said. "In fact, you shouldn't be goin' down there even in the daylight."

Rowena gather her wits enough to nod and after gulping, she said, "Daddy's right. You get lost down there you could step in a sink hole and you'd never be found."

They meant well, and they were honestly worried about me. I could see in their eyes. But, the swamp was the key to this whole mess, and I needed to see it for myself.

"I bought the equipment I need to get in and out safely," I said. "Don't worry."

"Yeah, but you don't know this swamp," Rowena said.

I shrugged. "I've had to go into a lot of places I didn't know, and believe me, most of them were a lot more dangerous than your swamp." I didn't mention that usually I at least had maps, satellite photos, or intelligence, but this wasn't a combat zone, so I wasn't worried that much.

"You mean when you were in the army? What did you do in the army?" Winston asked.

"Sorry, cuz, if I told you that I'd have to kill you." His eyes went wide. I smiled and waved my hands to let him know that I was kidding—sort of.

"I still wish you wouldn't do it," he said.

"At least, you ought to take someone with you," Rowena chimed in.

I shook my head. "No, I can move faster and quieter alone. Unless the person's been trained in this kind of operation, they just get in the way."

That was the end of the conversation. Neither of them was satisfied, but I can be pretty stubborn myself. After all, I'm originally from East Texas too, so I think I inherited the stubborn gene.

I didn't feel much like talking after dinner, and with my plan to visit the swamp, the idea of imbibing alcohol was a non-starter, so I excused myself, and left the two of them sitting in the living room with long-necked bottles of Lone Star beer in their hands and went to my room.

The window of my bedroom faced east. I drew back the curtains and looked outside. It was approaching 7:00 pm and the eastern sky was turning purple, still too light outside for me to be able to approach the swamp unseen, and I had a feeling that Dudley Jarvis was keeping an eye on approaches to the swamp. I figured it'd be dark enough by 10:00, which gave me time for a couple hours of shut-eye.

Before going to sleep, though, I had one more thing I had to do. I took my phone from my pocket and hit number 1 on speed dial.

"Hello, babe," Sandra's sleep voice said. "How are things in the Lone Star State?"

"Pretty lonely without you," I said. "You sound like you're getting ready for bed."

"Not much else to do without you around."

"I just wanted to hear your voice before I went to sleep. How was your day?"

"School's out, and I don't have a thing to do. I gave the house a good cleaning today, had a light supper, and thought I'd hit the pillow early. What about you, did you do anything interesting today?"

I gave her the short version of my day.

"What are you planning to do tonight?" she asked.

"Oh, just hit the rack and start again tomorrow," I said.

"Is it dangerous?"

"Is what dangerous?"

"What you're planning to do tonight?"

I hesitated. When I'm at home, she knows when I'm planning a night operation, because she sees me getting my gear together. From the slight quaver in her voice, that little tremor she gets every time I put on my black commando gear and strap my K-Bar knife in the ankle sheath I prefer. It was as if she was in the room with me.

"What makes you think I'm planning to do anything?"

"I don't know," she said. Her voice sounded weary. "I just *know*. Now, tell me, is it dangerous?"

It was a fair question, and one I hadn't asked myself really. Just how dangerous could it be? Snakes and alligators aren't exactly a walk in the park, but I'd been in far more dangerous situations, so I was pretty confident that I could handle it.

"No, it's not dangerous," I said. "It's just something I can't do in daylight. I need to check out the land they're trying to buy from my cousin, but I don't want anyone to know that I've done it."

There was a long moment of silence. Then, sounding a little less weary, her voice came back on, "Okay, babe, just be careful."

"It's just a little land reconnaissance. Nothing to worry about, really."

"Okay . . . I love you, you know."

"I love you, too, babe, now you get your beauty rest. I'll be seeing you in a few days."

I broke the connection, put the phone on the nightstand, and lay back on top of the covers. I was asleep almost instantly.

* * *

Two hours later, my eyes snapped open. I looked at my watch. The time was 9:15. I looked at the sky through the curtains I'd left open. The sky was inky black. It was time to rock and roll.

My duffel bag lay on the floor in the closet, still unpacked. I pulled it out and tossed it on the bed, and began dressing. Heavy-duty black cotton pants with Velcro pockets in the legs and reinforced belt loops, a long-sleeved black cotton shirt with chest pockets and pockets on both sleeves formed my basic uniform. I threaded a black, canvas web belt with a dull black clasp buckle through the pants' belt loops. My regular brown socks were replaced by a pair of black woolen socks with reinforced toes and heels, and over them I pulled the chest waders and hooked the straps over my shoulders.. Over my close-cropped hair—now starting to show a lot of gray I noted as I looked at my reflection in the mirror—I pulled on a black wool knit cap like skiers wear, but without the mask. I also have one that pulls down over my face, that has eye and nose holes, but I'd left that one home in my closet. If an alligator happened to spot me, I wouldn't have to worry about my description being passed along.

I then clipped the LED flashlight to a loop in one of the wader's pockets, and using a couple of black military blousing garters I'd picked up at an Army surplus store in Silver Spring, Maryland, secured my new K-Bar to my left forearm, double wrapping the garters before hooking the two ends together. It wasn't an ideal setup; I would have preferred strapping it to my ankle, but I knew I'd be doing a bit of wading, wasn't sure how deep the water would be, and wanted it near at hand at all times.

The final two items, my infrared flashlight and the alligator gig, I picked up off the floor, the gig held loosely in my right hand with the prongs down, looked around one last time, and headed out.

The house was quiet as I made my way downstairs and out through the kitchen. Outside, the sky was jet black with a few scattered pin pricks of stars. The dairy barn and chicken sheds were quiet. The only sounds were the chirrup of frogs and insects.

I crossed the back yard, past the chicken sheds and started walking through the fields, aiming toward the side of the swamp farthest from the Jarvis property line. I had a hunch that Dudley Jarvis kept a pretty close eye on the swamp to see who might come and go, and I wanted to avoid him—at least, for now. I had plans to confront him later.

The leaves of the corn stalks made rasping noises against my arms as I transited the corn field, but my passage through the rest of the fields was silent. I alternated between looking at the tree line, a darker, serrated shape against the dark of the sky, and to my left toward where Jarvis might be lurking, walking in a slight crouch to minimize the chance of being seen as a dark silhouette against the sky should he happen to be looking in that direction.

I made good time to the trees, and once inside the tree line, walked upright, keeping to the bare areas where the ground was soft and somewhat mushy. Under the trees, the darkness reminded me of patrols through triple canopy jungles, almost too dark to be able to see your hand when you held a foot away from your face, so I flicked on the infrared flashlight. Practically invisible from a distance, the broad beam illuminated a semi-circle in front of me in shades that ranged from inky black to a reddish-green, just enough to enable me to see where to put my foot without stepping on dead branches or into a hole, and hopefully enough to see a snake or gator in my path.

The swamp was anything but quiet. The closeness of the trees magnified sounds, and the deep croaking of frogs and the high-pitched whine of insects seemed to come at me from all directions. The rotten-egg smell, as bad as it had been when I'd approached the swamp previously, was ten times worse. It was so thick in the air I could feel it against my skin and crawling up my nostrils. It wrapped around me like a wet wool blanket.

I walked until the burbling sound of a slow-flowing stream joined the noises of the wildlife. From the volume of sound, I was less than twenty feet from the stream that marked the boundary of the swamp and Winston's land. I veered left and started moving in a lazy zig-zag pattern toward the Jarvis farm. Near the stream it was mostly boggy pools, some up to two feet deep, slowing my progress as I waded through them. There were several hummocks of relatively dry ground, irregular mounds of earth from which sprouted evergreens, willows and cypress trees, covered with moss or what looked like a miniature version of Southeast Asia's elephant grass. Some of the mounds weren't much bigger than a pool table, and some were fifty or more feet across. I didn't see any animals, but I could hear things slithering through the grass.

Going was slow, especially when I waded through the pools, where I was extra cautious to keep from making splashing noises, partly to keep from being heard, and partly to keep from attracting the attention of a hungry alligator. A quick glance at my watch showed me that I'd been walking for just over an hour, and still I figured I wasn't even halfway across the swamp. Worse, I'd seen nothing in the red-hued highlights and ebony shadows that gave me the slightest clue as to what it was about this place that attracted Caldwell. Added to all that, the stench was making my eyes water, and I was beginning to taste it, and that was an extremely unpleasant situation. Too much longer, and it wouldn't be the gators or Jarvis who did me in, the swamp itself would be my undoing. I chuckled as I imagined the coroner's report, 'subject died from an excess of stink.'

I resolved to give it another half hour, which should put me about midway, and then I'd call it a night.

About five minutes later, a flicker far to my front caught my eye. I was on one of the hummocks, a little rounded hill about five feet in diameter with two pine trees on it. I stopped near the tallest of the two trees, turned off my infrared right as a precaution, and peered into the darkness. The light was an indistinct blob that swayed slightly and looked to be coming nearer. With nothing to measure it against I couldn't accurately estimate the distance to it, but my inability to hear any sound coming from that direction meant it had to be a hundred or more yards away—assuming, that is, that it was something that made sound.

Now, at this point you're probably thinking that I'd considered ghosts as one possibility to explain the mysterious light, but nothing could be farther from the truth. A number of possibilities flitted through my mind; swamp gas, a swarm of lightning bugs, or someone walking through the swamp carrying a lantern or flashlight. The lack of any sense of a 'beam' of light, made me settle on lantern, and the rational part of my mind told me that this was someone trekking through the muck and mire just like me. Furthermore, it had to be around two hundred yards from me, could, in fact, be a bit farther away, but even so, that meant that whoever it was, they were on Winston's property.

I thought of Dudley Jarvis and his shotgun and clutched the alligator gig more tightly. For a moment I debated slipping through the woods to get a look at the cause of the mysterious light, but I saw those double barrels in my mind, and realized that in the dark, the gun had all the advantages. Never carry a knife to a gunfight, and don't face a shotgun with an oversized fork.

I turned and began retracing my steps. Exploring the swamp at night turned out not to be one of my better ideas.

Even though I hadn't seen him, I was pretty sure it had been Dudley Jarvis with that light prowling through the swamp. What on earth would draw him into that foul-smelling place that late at night? Then, I remembered that we sat astride the main smuggling route for contraband and drugs from Mexico bound for points north. I was also aware that drug use, everything from cocaine to meth-amphetamines, was on the rise in rural regions. It made sense. If Dudley Jarvis was involved in smuggling, he'd need a safe place to hold goods until he could arrange transportation. What better place than a fetid, foul-smelling swamp that no one wanted to enter, *and* on someone else's land to boot.

Of course, that also meant he was likely to have accomplices, and be prepared to use deadly force to protect his little operation.

I could always just report it to the local law enforcement authorities, but if I was wrong, I'd be souring relations between Winston and his neighbor. I had to be absolutely sure.

So, it was back to the drawing board.

Chapter 14

His heart beat so strongly against his chest walls he was sure the boy could hear it. He licked his lips in anticipation, and clenched his fists to hide the way his hands trembled.

My God, he thought, he looks just *like* Joshua. As if he'd been reincarnated.

Of course, he didn't really believe in reincarnation. Despite what his father and the preachers said, he believed that the only thing that waited when you died was eternal blackness, nothingness, a void from which there was no escape. Maybe there was a heaven, but hell, he knew now, was right here on earth. Heaven he imagined as a great void, where souls wandered until they found another kindred soul.

His Joshua was in that void. If the hereafter existed, maybe someday he would join him there. They could finally be together they way they'd promised each other all those years ago.

They'd been barely more than children then, on the cusp of manhood. That time when you think you're immortal and there's nothing ahead of you but all the time in the world.

* * *

It was mid-August, and their chores were done, so they'd gone down to the stream to cool off. They'd stripped down to their skivvies and swam, and were laying on the soft grass next to the stream letting the afternoon sun dry their bodies.

He couldn't keep his eyes off Joshua. Nor, at first, could he understand the strange feelings he experienced as he watched the play of muscles beneath his friend's golden brown skin, or the fact that whenever Joshua smiled at him, he found that he could hardly breathe.

They lay side by side, not touching, but close enough that he could feel the heat emanating from Joshua's body.

It wasn't the first time. It had begun months before when they'd been working alone in the barn. After completing the tasks his father had assigned them, they'd begun horsing around. Their wrestling and tumbling in the hayloft turned into something else, and they'd taken every opportunity since that day to find time alone together.

After a month, they'd finally found the courage to talk about it, and admit the way they felt about each other. They'd decided that at the end of August, just before school started, they would run away, maybe out to

California, because they'd heard that their kind was at least tolerated out there.

His mind kept going back to that day, that hot, humid, fateful August day. Their hands had brushed against each other, followed by arms, and then . . . and then . . . just as their bodies came together, a dark shadow blotted out the sun.

His father, a stormy expression on his sun-burned, leathery face, looked down at him. His mouth was moving, but the sounds that came out, garbled and mixed with flying globules of spit, were unintelligible.

Before his brain could register his father's presence, he saw a flash before his eyes, felt a pain in his left shoulder, and sensed that the world was moving past him at an alarming rate, a cacophony of sensations that resolved into him being yanked from the ground, his father's gnarled hands grasping his left bicep in a vice-like grip. He was flung aside as casually as one would toss a pine cone, coming to rest face down, in a daze, in the soft earth of the stream's bank. It took him a few seconds to recover his wits and his vision to clear. He saw his father, bent at the waist, raising and lowering the heavy, carved wooden cane that he had to use often now, grunting each time he lowered it in a slashing motion.

Streamers of red, the late afternoon sunlight glittering off them, sprayed out in lazy arcs each time the cane came down.

His vision was just clearing as his father, with one last 'hmph!', slammed the cane down. Shoulders slumped, he turned and advanced toward him. He just had time to raise an arm to ward off the blow as the cane crashed down against his forearm. The pain, like a white-hot flame, flared up his arm and throughout his body. He opened his mouth to scream, but his father took a step backwards and held up a commanding hand, "Shut your mouth, boy." He pointed with the cane at the dark lump near the stream. "You start cryin', and I'll do to you what I done to that niggah. I oughta do it anyway." Flies were already beginning to swarm around the blood-covered bundle which was hardly recognizable as . . . Joshua.

His hand flew to his mouth, and he fought to hold back the contents of his stomach, but failed. Acidic green bile spewed from his mouth.

His father's lips curled downward. "I guess I can't expect nothin' better from a sissy like you." He spat, the globule of brown tobacco juice landed near his feet. "Now, you git yo faggoty ass up and you git rid of that body, and you git rid of it good, you hear." With one last look of disdain, he swirled and, jabbing his cane into the soft earth, walked away.

When his stomach settled, he did as his father had ordered. He put his Joshua in a safe place where no one could find him, no one could disturb his final resting place.

* * *

For a year, he didn't speak of it; hardly spoke to his father other than a grunt of assent when the old man ordered him to do some chore or other. But, he never forgot. He wasn't sure he'd ever believed in God or an afterlife, and wondered if maybe he'd been wrong. He was sure that Joshua would be waiting for him in some heavenly place when he too died. He'd even considered killing himself, but simply couldn't summon up the courage.

Then, one day, almost a year to the day later, he'd spotted the young black boy walking along the road as he was coming back from town. The boy reminded him of Joshua, and the memories came flooding back.

He'd stopped and offered him a ride. As they rode they talked, and he learned that the boy was from a family of sharecroppers recently arrived in the area from Louisiana, and he'd become tired of the back-breaking, sunup to sundown work, so he'd decided to run away to Houston. He sympathized with him, and gave him one of the bottles of Royal Crown cola from the cooler he kept in the bed of the pickup. He then invited the boy to join him for lunch near the stream.

Once they arrived at the stream and he'd given the boy another cola and one of his bologna sandwiches, baloney sam'ich the boy had called it, they sat shoulder to shoulder on the bank watching the glitter of sunlight off the water.

Talking turned to touching and soon they were mostly unclothed, lying in the grass.

When his work-hardened hands clasped the boy's throat, the look of curiosity in his eyes turned to fear. The boy began to buck and wiggle, but he was no match in size or strength, and it was over almost before it started.

He gazed down lovingly as the life faded from the boy's deep brown eyes.

Finally, he knelt over the small body, caressing the smooth cheeks, tears streaming down his craggy cheeks.

"Don't you fret, Joshua," he said in a choked voice. "I'm gon' bring you somebody to keep you company 'till it's my turn. You won't be alone no more."

Chapter 15

Back at the farmhouse I stripped the waders off and, using the hose attached to the spigot at the back door, washed the mud off as best I could. The putrid smell of the swamp, though, had somehow seeped through the waterproof material and permeated my shirt and trousers, or for all I know, it had the capability to ignore the rubber of the waders and go through it like water through tissue paper.

I stripped shirt and trousers off, rolled them up and dumped them on the ground near the coiled up hose. After hanging the waders over the propane tank, I grabbed the gator gig and my K-Bar and made my way in stockinged feet through the kitchen, upstairs to my room, where I got clean underwear and went across the hall to the bathroom and took a long shower.

I was coming out of the bathroom with my dirty underwear just as Rowena came out of her bedroom. She was dressed in leg-hugging pajama pants and a flower-print tee shirt, her hair stuck out in all directions, and the left side of her face was furrowed. She was yawning, and gulped, almost choking, when she saw me standing there in my boxer shirts and tee shirt. Then, she made a face and pinched her nostrils closed.

"Phew! You smell like you've been rolling around in a pig pen," she said.

I quickly sniffed at my underarms, only to realize that what she smelled wasn't me, but the underwear I was carrying.

"Sorry," I said. "The odor of that swamp really clings to clothing." I put the hand holding the offending articles behind my back.

"Oh, yeah, how'd that little trip go?"

"It was a bust, I'm afraid. I'll have to go back during daylight, because you can't really see diddly at night, even with a flashlight." I decided to leave out the moving light and my suspicions about Jarvis.

"Hmph, I could've told you that. Hey, what time is it?"

"Time for you to go back to bed, and just time enough for me to get a few hours' sleep before breakfast."

She yawned again and scratched her midsection. "Uh huh, but I got to pee first." She brushed past me and entered the bathroom.

I could hear the sound of water splashing into the toilet as I beat a hasty retreat to my room.

* * *

Despite having less than six hours' sleep, I felt refreshed at breakfast with Winston and Rowena. She made no mention of our late night encounter, while Winston listened with feigned interest as I told them of my trip to the swamp, again leaving out any reference to seeing the light, or what I suspected that light meant. I was pretty sure that had to be Jarvis, but until I had a better idea of his fixation on the swamp, I thought I'd keep it to myself. I wasn't sure what Winston might do if he knew that the man was coming onto his property in the dead of night, but I had an idea that it might involve damage to Jarvis's anatomy, which would get Winston in trouble, or worse, if Jarvis *was* involved in smuggling.

After breakfast, I informed them that I was driving to Lufkin to check on something. That something was Global Energy, but that too was a detail that I kept to myself. Winston was preoccupied with some kind of fungus he'd found in one of the chicken sheds, and Rowena blushed each time I looker her way— probably still embarrassed that I'd seen her not at her best—so neither of them questioned me about details.

I dressed in jeans, a plaid shirt, and the shoes I'd worn on the flight from DC. A tan windbreaker would have to substitute for a suit coat, something I reserved for funerals, weddings, or meetings with the mayors of major cities, and I had yet to meet with a mayor.

By 8:00 I was behind the wheel of the 4-Runner heading for Lufkin. The northbound traffic on U.S. 69 was light until I got to within ten miles of Lufkin, when the inbound commuter traffic from the surrounding small towns picked up. There were lots of semis, some with livestock trailers, oil tankers and pickup trucks, and the occasional van or sedan. I entered the outskirts of the city at 9:05.

Heather had given me the address and directions to Global Energy, but I didn't really need them.

The company was in a huge steel, glass and concrete building in Lufkin's southeast, five stories tall and about two city blocks by two city blocks, it sat in the center of a large fenced area that was mostly a blacktop parking lot with a few green spaces with picnic tables and benches interspersed here and there. It sat next to a large John Deere tractor dealership, which was an open field with hundreds of tractors and other farm vehicles parked around a modest sized one story prefab aluminum building.

There were two entry gates, one in the center of the fence with a big sign that said 'Employees Only!,' and another near the tractor dealership marked 'Visitors.' I pulled up to the 'Visitors' guard booth. A portly rent-a-cop with a belly that reached my car two feet before the rest of his body and obscured his belt buckle, inquired my reason for visiting, nodded when I said I was there to see Loren Caldwell, and waved me in. I found an empty parking space in the far corner and walked what felt like a mile to the entrance.

Two guards stood outside the big glass double doors watching those entering and exiting, and they were definitely *not* your usual rent-a-cops. Their blue uniform shirts bulged in places that said these guys did some serious time in a gym with free weights on a regular basis, and the unblinking, steely looks they gave people as they passed marked them as ex-military, probably special operations. The one to my right blinked and narrowed his eyes at me as I walked past, probably recognizing me as former military as well. Funny how that works. Former military people recognize each other much like American tourists abroad recognized each other. Usually, these encounters are friendly, but I got a sense from these two that wasn't the case here. I probably wouldn't have liked them if I met them while they were still in uniform either.

The lobby was a wide, taking up the center third of the building and reaching all the way to the back. Glass walls from the entry doors funneled everyone toward a large desk on the right. As they reached the desk, some people flashed badges and were directed to the left end, while those of us without badges, which was me, had to go through in inquisition; name, address, who we were there to visit, and reason for visit, and then show a photo ID—I showed the dead-eyed guy behind the desk my Maryland Driver's License—given an 'Escort Required' badge on a metal necklace and instructed to keep it visible at all times. I was then directed to a grouping of plush chairs grouped around a low glass-top table and told that someone would be with me directly.

I took a seat facing the big glass front of the building, but from where I could also see the check-in desk and the wall facing it, in which there were several doors, through one of which I expected my escorts would come. It would have been nice to get a glimpse of them, him, or her before I was spotted, but the cameras mounted high up on the walls, most facing the check-in desk, had probably already recorded my image. At least, I'd see them coming—I hoped.

There were magazines and newspapers scattered artfully atop the glass table, *Sports Illustrated, Readers' Digest, The Houston Chronicle, The Dallas Morning News, The Wall Street Journal* and several magazines related to the energy industry. Whether they were there for the edification of visitors, or because waiting times were long was totally irrelevant to me, as I didn't want to read any of them. At 10:02 I picked up *Reader's Digest*. It was the May issue. I began reading at the front, and by 10:30 had made my way halfway through, and worn the last thread of my patience thin. If this was an example of the way Global Energy handled customers there was no wonder their stock was tanking.

I was just about to toss the magazine back onto the table when the door in the center of the far wall opened and three men stepped into the lobby.

The man in the middle was tall, about six-one, with the narrow hips and broad shoulders of a running back. Close-cropped blond hair, chiseled features, and expensive gray suit couldn't mask the fact that he, like the guards at the front, was a former GI. Flanking him were two goons who looked like they'd been stamped from the same mold. Broad shoulders, dark jackets straining to hold them in, and bulges indicating large firearms, they walked close to the center guy, but far enough to allow quick and unimpeded movement if needed. Their haircuts were close, high and tight the Marine Corps call it, and the color was sandy brown. Topping off the gangster look were dark wraparound sunglasses worn indoors.

They stopped and gray suit looked toward the reception desk and then at me. He made a beeline for where I sat, with Frick and Frack still flanking, but slightly behind, their eyes roaming around taking in the entire space. They might look like two-bit gangsters, but they knew what they were doing.

Gray suit stopped six feet away and stared down at me. Frick and Frack were three feet further back, pretending to ignore me. But, I wasn't fooled by that. I could tell that both of them kept me in their peripheral vision, and stood so that should I try anything they had clear lines of fire without risk to each other or gray suit. These guys were stone hard pros, and I wondered why the hell an energy company needed this kind of muscle.

"Mr. Pennyback?" Gray suit asked.

"Yeah, that's me," I said. "And, you are?"

His eyes narrowed and a muscle in his jaw twitched. He wasn't used to people not jumping when he spoke. "I'm Alan Grayson, chief of security. Who are you here to see?"

"When they called you, they told you my name, and they didn't tell you why I'm here? You need to fire your receptionist."

Now, his lips clenched so hard they turned white. He was playing a game, and I'd just refused to play.

"You'd like to speak with . . . Loren Caldwell . . . was that the name you gave the guard at reception?"

"Yes, I'd like to speak to Loren Caldwell. Does he work here?"

He looked at me like you'd look at a smear of dog crap on the bottom of your shoe. Then, almost too quick to be noticed if I hadn't been looking closely at him, his eyes darted to the right and back at me. His expression changed. It was like I was looking at a wooden statue. Then, his lips moved.

"We had a Loren Caldwell here at Global Energy," he said. His voice lacked any trace of feeling. "He quit over a year ago."

"Do you have any idea how I might contact him?"

"Even if we did, privacy laws would prevent me from sharing such information with you," he said. Again, the flicker of the eyes. "Why do you wish to speak to Mr. Caldwell?"

"It's a personal matter," I said. I stood and faced him. Our eyes were on the same level, but I think he might've had five or ten pounds on me. "Thank you for your time, Mr. Grayson."

I didn't offer to shake hands, and neither did he.

"You're welcome, Mr. Pennyback," he said. "Good luck finding Mr. Caldwell."

He turned and walked back to the door through which he'd come. Frick and Frack fell in behind him, still scanning the space like little wind-up toys with only one setting. I turned and headed for the exit.

He hadn't sound like he meant it when he wished me good luck. Of course, he didn't wish me good luck. Alan Grayson had been lying to me. Caldwell had lied to me.

But, I knew where I could get some answers.

Charles Ray

Chapter 16

With a stop about halfway at a tin-roofed barbecue shack just off U.S. 69 to grab a pulled pork sandwich and a glass of unsweetened iced tea, it took me two hours to get back to Poseyville. It was 3:30 when I pulled into a parking space at the Bide a While motel.

The same thin-faced, flat-chested woman was behind the reception desk, only looking bored and ready to go home this time. She gave me a weak smile as I entered the lobby, a look of confusion when I veered left instead of approaching the desk, and then a nod when I pointed to the hallway leading to the conference centers.

The same woman was sitting outside Caldwell's office. She was painting her nails. She looked up and smiled when I entered the office.

"If you're looking for Mr. Caldwell," she said. "He's out of the office and not expected back for a while." She kept painting her nails.

"Actually, I was hoping I could have a word with you," I said.

A worried expression flickered quickly on her face. She stopped painting her nails and carefully replaced the brush in the bottle and set it aside.

"I remember you; you were in yesterday, right?" I nodded. "Like I told you then, I don't really know a lot about the business. I just answer the phone and greet visitors, and get coffee."

Beads of sweat popped out above her upper lip, and she kept her gaze fixed on the nail polish bottle.

"You probably know more than you think you know," I said. She looked scared, but I believed her when she said she didn't know what Caldwell was up to. I decided to take a chance. "Look, I think your boss is trying to cheat my cousin out of his land. I'd just like to ask you a few questions about things you've seen and heard; things you might not have given a second thought to, but that might be important. For instance, are you familiar with Global Energy?"

She shook her head. "No, I . . . well, I did hear—" Her eyes darted from the entrance door to the door to Caldwell's office.

"You heard what?"

"Look, I can't talk to you here," she said in a voice just above a whisper. "I don't know when Mr. Caldwell might come back, and he might not like me talking to you." She looked at me finally. I could see fear in her eyes, but there was something else, too, that I couldn't interpret. "If you could come back at 5:00 when I get off and follow me to my house."

"Okay, I'll meet you here at 5:00."

The panicked look came back. "No, not here! Wait for me . . . in front of the barbecue place on the main street. Do you know it?" I nodded again. "I'm driving a blue Honda Civic, you can't miss it, and I'll be driving real slow. When you see me, fall in behind and follow me. I live outside town, and my nearest neighbor's half a mile away."

"I'm driving a silver Toyota 4-Runner. It's a rental," I said. "I'll keep an eye out for you, but drive like you normally would. I wouldn't want you drawing attention to yourself. When you pass me, I'll pull in behind and blink my lights twice so you'll know it's me."

"Okay, I'll see you at 5:00."

"By the way, my name's Al Pennyback," I said.

"I'm Nancy Jo Billings," she said.

"What do your friends call you, Nancy or Jo?"

"Nancy Jo."

Of course. I forgot this was Texas.

"All right, Nancy Jo," I said. "I'll see you at 5:00. Remember, when you see lights behind you flash twice, that'll be me."

"I got it." Her brow wrinkled as she frowned. "I'm not dumb."

"I don't think you're dumb." I actually did. "When I was in the army, though, we always repeated orders to make sure we had them down cold. Old habits die hard."

"Well, I do remember. I drive normal and you'll blink your lights twice and then follow me home. Don't take a rocket scientist to figure that out."

She looked relieved when I turned to leave.

* * *

With over an hour to kill, I drove to Winston's place and changed into black pants, black shirt, and black boots. I wanted to be prepared just in case things ran late and some more night work was required. Without the waders, it was easier to strap the K-Bar to my ankle with the handle just far enough up above the top of my boots for me to easily grasp it. For good measure, I took both flashlights and the gator gig, which I tossed into the 4-Runner's back seat.

I was back in downtown Poseyville by 4:45, and parked across the street from the barbecue joint. I'd originally planned to park in one of the empty spots directly in front of the place, but on the drive back into town I realized that I'd not asked Nancy Jo which direction she'd be turning when she came off the street from the Bide a While. By parking across the street, where I could watch the intersection, I'd be able to see her car and either pull out and follow, or make a U-turn and do the same.

Luck was with me. She made a left at the intersection, so all I had to do was pull out and pull up about two car lengths behind. I flicked my headlights on and off twice, and cringed when she waved. She was clearly not cut out for clandestine operations.

She did, however, take my advice about driving normally, or at least what passed as normal for locals, twenty miles an hour over the limit. Even at fifty-five it took us thirty minutes to reach her place. She lived in an old farm house, surrounded by lots of land and stands of trees, and not another house in sight. The drive from the street to the packed-earth yard in front of the two-story white frame house was almost a quarter mile, perfectly straight, so no one could drive up to the house without being seen. She stopped near the steps leading up to the wrap-around front porch, and I pulled in behind her.

By the time I got out of my vehicle she was waiting for me at the bottom of the steps. When I joined her she was smiling and her cheeks were flushed.

"I feel just like one of those secret agents," she said. She turned and went up the steps to the porch. "Come on in."

I followed her into a large living room, with old but tasteful furnishings. White lace doilies draped over the arm of a sofa and love seat that dominated the room. Across the room, facing the sofa, was a large credenza. She walked to the credenza and lifted a lid in the center.

"Would you like a drink? I have bourbon, gin, and tequila, or if you'd prefer beer, I have Budweiser in the fridge."

"What are you having?"

She took a bottle of *Jose Cuervo Especial* and two tumblers from the credenza and set them aside. "I'm partial to tequila myself," she said.

"Then, I'll have the same."

"Okay." She pointed toward the sofa. "Make yourself comfortable, while I get salt and limes from the kitchen."

The fake leather of the sofa cushions was cracked, and the pad made a whooshing sound as I sat. But, the place was neat.

She walked in a few minutes later carrying a large salt shaker and a bowl filled with lime wedges, which she put on the rectangular coffee table in front of the sofa. She then retrieved the tequila and glasses and joined me on the sofa. Watching me out of the side of her eye, she opened the bottle and poured half an inch of the viscous liquor into each glass. She handed me one glass.

"You familiar with the traditional Mexican way of drinking tequila?" she asked. "I learned it two years ago when one of my girlfriends and I visited the Yucatan."

I nodded. "I am," I said. "Although, the *Los Angeles Times*, back in the 1920s described it a little different from the way it's done today."

Her left eyebrow arched upwards. "Oh, how is that?"

"Well, instead of licking the salt, drinking the tequila, and sucking a lime, they said you suck a lemon and then drink the tequila."

She made a face like she'd just sucked a lemon. "Ee-e-ew, that doesn't sound sexy at all. I like the way they showed us."

To demonstrate, she licked the back of her hand to moisten it, sprinkled on some salt on the moist spot, and then licked it off. Lifting the glass, she downed the oily tequila in one big gulp, and then picked a lime from the bowl and clamped it between her lips, sucking hard. She made 'ooh' sounds as she sucked.

I copied her actions, except for downing the entire contents of the glass. 'Down the hatch' has never been one of my favorite toasts. I put my glass, still containing half of what she'd poured in, on the coffee table. She reached for the bottle, but I gently grasped her wrist.

"How about we have a little talk before you drink too much?"

She batted her lashes at me, but didn't pull her hand back. "Aw, can't a girl have a little fun? I can hold my liquor, you know."

"Of that I have no doubt," I said. "But, I'm not sure I can, and it wouldn't be polite for me to sit here and let you drink alone."

She put her glass down, and laid her free hand on mine, gently massaging as she gazed into my eyes. Another good reason for me to limit my alcohol intake; I had a feeling that her mind was going in a direction I didn't want to go, and I'd need to be sharp-witted to be able to let her down without offending her.

"Okay, if you insist." She shrugged, and let her hand linger on mine for several seconds after I released my hold on her wrist. "What do you want to know?"

"At your office you were about to say something about Global Energy, what was that?"

"It wasn't exactly Global *Energy* I heard, but one day, when I was taking Mr. Caldwell his coffee, he was on the phone, and I heard him say 'Global will come out smelling like a rose on these deals.' Do you think he might've been talking about Global Energy?"

"I'd bet money he was." I nodded. "Do you have any idea what these deals were?"

She scrunched her eyes shut and leaned back on the sofa.

"You're gonna think I'm a bad person if I tell you that," she said.

"Why would I do that? You'd be helping me help my cousin."

"Yeah, there is that. Well, it's like this. One day, Mr. Caldwell was out somewhere, and a courier delivered an envelope for him. I went in to put it on his desk, and I know it's wrong to snoop, but there were some folders out on his desk, and I took a peek."

"What was in the folders?"

"Not much," she said. "Just a few plat maps and copies of deeds. One of them was your cousin, Winston Jones."

Not necessarily a smoking gun. Caldwell was, after all, trying to buy a chunk of my cousin's land.

"Do you remember anything from any of the other folders?"

"Not a lot." She shook her head. "There was one other name that I remember, though, because he's a neighbor. Angus Murphy. He owns the farm adjacent to mine. There was the same papers in that folder, too."

I tried to process what she'd just said. My cousin's property was on the other side of town. Why would Caldwell be interested in such widely separated plots of land? There was only way to find out.

"Do you think this Angus Murphy's at home?"

"He's a farmer, so he's usually there if he's not taking crops to market, or in town buying supplies. Why?"

"I think I need to pay him a visit."

She laid a well-manicured hand on my thigh and leaned in close so that our legs were touching. I could feel the heat of her body against my leg, and a tingle when she brushed her fingers against my thigh.

"Surely there's no hurry," she said, her voice low and husky. "Angus isn't going anywhere."

I took hold of her hand and lifted it slowly from my thigh. This was the tricky part; disengaging without alienating. I lifted her hand to my lips and lightly kissed the tips of her fingers.

"Nancy Jo, you're a beautiful woman," I said. "And, any other time, I'd be flattered by your attentions. Hell, I'm flattered now . . . but, I'm in a committed relationship, and letting this go any further wouldn't be fair to either of us."

She grasped my hand with both of hers and pulled it against her ample chest. I could feel her heart beating. She had a wistful look on her face.

"Damnit, all the really good men seem to be already taken. I'm jealous of this woman who has the key to your heart," she said. "And, I hope she knows just how lucky she is."

With my free hand I brushed away a lock of hair that had fallen over her left eye.

"You're a beautiful woman. Trust me, you'll find someone."

After getting directions to Angus Murphy's house, I kissed her on the forehead and left. In my rearview mirror I could see her standing at the top of the porch steps watching me leave, and I wondered how many times she'd done that in her life.

I felt bad. Not about resisting her advances; I'd made a commitment to Sandra, and was determined to keep it; but because

I'd used her, and hadn't even bothered to learn anything about her. I'd been just another ripple in the stream, intersecting with her life and moving on.

Chapter 17

A ngus Murphy's house was considerably farther from the main road than Nancy Jo's, reached by a winding dirt road that was little more than tire tracks in the reddish clay, with limp grass growing in the middle. The barbed wire fence at the entrance was rusted, and strands had come loose from the weathered and peeling fence posts.

The house, when I made the last turn in the dirt road and it came into view, looked as rundown as the fence. It had once been white, but the side boards were now gray and streaked. There were several slates missing from the green roof, and the yard was mostly red clay, with a few clumps of saw grass, and old, rotted tires scattered about. The front porch had once been screened in, but huge gaps in the screen hadn't been repaired.

An old man, as gaunt as a scarecrow, wearing tattered overalls and scuffed brown boots, stood at the top of the uneven porch steps, holding a battered gray Stetson in his right hand while he ran his left through was left of his stringy gray hair. His craggy, sun-browned face looked like an old paper map that had been folded and refolded so many times the creases had become permanent. He was of that indeterminate age, could have been anywhere from seventy to ninety. I pegged him at the high side of that range.

I pulled up near the porch, cut the engine, and got out.

"You must be Mr. Pennyback," he said as I approached. "Nancy Jo called and said you was comin' over."

He thrust out a gnarled hand as I reached the steps. Up close, he looked even older, but his grip was dry and strong.

"I hope I'm not intruding, Mr. Murphy, dropping in unannounced like this."

"Never you mind, young fella. Ain't nobody here but me, and truth be told, I could use the compn'y. Come on in the house and set a spell."

I followed him in, stepping gingerly on the uneven boards of the steps, over a gap in the floorboards of the porch and into a living room that looked like a tornado had hit it. The upholstery on the sofa and recliner in the center of the room was frayed and full of holes and cigarette burns, and the wooden coffee table, leaning with one leg bent inwards, was scarred and buckled and covered with circular watermarks and four dirty plates with the crust of partially-eaten meals in various states of petrification.

Empty and partially empty whiskey bottles lay beside the recliner, along with an overturned glass. The room smelled of sweat, rotting food, and stale liquor. I breathed as shallowly as possible.

"Forgive the mess," he said. "I ain't much for cleaning since the wife died five years ago."

Some of the plates looked like they'd been sitting there since the lady of the house passed, too.

"I know how that is. I remember being at sixes and sevens when my wife . . . died." I wasn't comfortable talking about Sara, but the look of understanding in his watery blue eyes told me that I'd said the right thing; I'd established common ground.

"Look, why don't you try'n find a clean place on the divan and set yourself down. I was about to pour myself a tipple; care to join me?"

After having drunk tequila with Nancy Jo Billings the last thing I needed was to pour more alcohol into my system. But, the social protocol in the South is pretty straight forward, when someone offers you food or drink, it's a serious insult to refuse. I remembered my Special Forces training at Fort Bragg, North Carolina as a young lieutenant. During the final weeks, my qualification class had to do a multi-day unconventional warfare exercise in the Uwharrie National Forest north of the fort. Locals from the small towns in and around the forest, in the spare times between tending their crops, came out and joined us, playing partisans and guerrilla bands in our war exercises. One of their rituals for each new team deployed, after linking up with their assigned partisan band, was to offer each team member a Mason jar of the local moonshine. The stuff smelled like kerosene and burned like hell going down your throat, but you had to drain the entire pint if you wanted their cooperation. This was billed as indoctrinating us to possible cultural practices in faraway countries to which we might be deployed, but it was an integral part of the local culture as well. In Murphy's case, it was even more important that I go along. For a white man of his generation to offer to share a drink with a black man was . . . significant.

"Sure," I said. "I'll have one. Just a little, though. I'm driving."

He chuckled. "You just have a seat, and I'll fetch the jug and some clean glasses."

He was back in less than a minute with a narrow-neck gallon jug containing what looked like water, and two 'clean' glasses; clean, in that they weren't fly-specked. He sat in the recliner, put the glasses on the coffee table and filled both them to near the brim. I found a relatively intact cushion at the end of the sofa near him and sat. He handed me a glass and held the other up in a toast.

"You might wanta toss it down fast," he said. "It burns less that way."

He lifted his glass to his lips and tilted his head back, draining half the liquid in a few swallows.

I lifted my glass to my lips. The smell wasn't too bad, a bit antiseptic, and up close, I could see the way light was refracted by the glass's contents. It clearly wasn't water. I tilted the glass and took a generous swallow—and, almost gagged.

It was like licking a hot stove, so hot the inside of my mouth went numb, burned my throat on the way down, and sat in my stomach like a hot tennis ball. I sucked air in and blew it out.

"Whew! That is some strong stuff," I said.

"Make it myself from the corn I grow." He finished draining his glass and refilled it. "Now, Nancy Jo said you wanted to talk to me 'bout this fella from up to Lufkin who's down here buying up worthless land?"

He didn't seem to mind that I'd only taken one drink, so I'd passed the social test. I was accepted.

"Yes. I understand he offered to buy some of your land."

"Sure nuff did," he said. "Fifteen acres of mostly marsh down to the southeast corner of my place. Won't nothin' grow there but snakes and sedge, but he don't seem to mind. Offered me a hundred fifty thousand for it "

Sounded like ten thousand an acre was the standard offering price. That made sense. If he offered someone more or less, in a small town like this, word would get around. This way, everyone would feel they were getting the same treatment, making it sound like a square deal.

"Did he say why he wanted it?"

"Something 'bout diggin' down to see what it was like in olden times. I didn't understand half of what he said, and frankly, I didn't give a shit. That's too much damn money to pass up."

"You agreed to sell?"

"Sure's hell did. I wasn't doin' nothin' with that piece of land anyway. Figured I might's well get *some* use out of it."

"Do you know if anyone else around here agreed to sell?"

"I think he said Moss Tucker over to the other end of town sold, but he still waitin' on three other people. I reckon he got a problem with Winston Jones. That fella Caldwell said he was bein' stubborn. 'Course, that don't surprise me. Old Winston's 'bout as stubborn as a mule, and he pretty attached to that place of his, it bein' in his family for so long'n all."

Somehow, it didn't surprise me that Murphy would know Winston. Poseyville wasn't all that big, and I knew one thing for sure, in small towns news traveled at the speed of light.

"Did it strike you as odd that Caldwell would want to pay so much for land that's essentially worthless?"

"Well, sure it did, son," he said. "I mean, he offered me five times the market price for land you can grow stuff on. But, I also ain't one to look a gift horse in the mouth. If he wants to pay me good money for bottom land what won't even grow cane, that's his problem."

"Has he paid you yet?"

"Naw. He ain't brought the papers for me to sign yet. Said he'd be doin' it 'round a week or so, and I'd get my money 'bout three or four weeks after that."

I found myself warming to this old codger. An uncomplicated man of the soil, he'd seen an opportunity and was grabbing for it. But, I had this itchy feeling that he was being cheated.

"Look, Mr. Murphy," I said. "It's none of my business what you do with your land, but you might want to hold off a bit on signing those papers."

"Why's that, son?"

"I think Caldwell's misrepresenting himself. There's no such organization as GeoSync, and I believe he works for Global Energy. I can't prove it yet, but I think, despite what seems like a generous offer, he's really cheating you."

His eyes went wide and he took another gulp of moonshine.

"You mean he work for one of them oil companies? You think maybe I got oil on my land?"

"I don't know yet, but I intend to find out." I rose. "One thing before I go. Do you know Dudley Jarvis?"

His eyes narrowed. "Yeah, I know him. Know that no-good daddy of his, too. Why?"

"They're neighbors of my cousin, Winston Jones, and they're objecting to Winston selling to Caldwell. Do you know of any reason that would bother them?"

"Nary a one. Now, mind you, them Jarvis's don't socialize much with folks in Poseyville, even though they been here long's I can remember, so I don't know how they even found out about this here fella, Caldwell, buying the land in the first place, less'n they's jealous 'bout your cousin gettin' an offer and they didn't."

While that was very possible—in fact, it was something I should have thought at first to check out—but, I couldn't escape the nagging feeling that there was something else going on.

I thanked Angus Murphy for his time and the drink—which I could still taste in the back of my throat—and drove back to Winston's.

Chapter 18

The combined effects of Nancy Jo's tequila and Angus Murphy's white lightning forced me to drive with extra caution; and despite that I weaved all over the road; left me with a headache, a numb feeling in my mouth, and a sour stomach. Consequently, supper with Winston and Rowena was a subdued affair. Once I explained to them where I'd been and what I'd done they thankfully kept conversation to a minimum. Immediately after supper, I took a long hot shower and crawled under the bed covers. I think I fell asleep right away, one of the only advantages of drinking too much.

I woke up the next morning with a slight ache at my temples and a mouth that felt like someone had stuffed it full of cotton. Rowena's breakfast of scrambled eggs, chicken-fried steak, hockey-puck-size biscuits, and home fried potatoes, washed down with freshly-brewed Maxwell House coffee, though, helped ease the pain and erased most of the nasty taste in my mouth.

After breakfast, Winston went out to do his usual chores, and I helped Rowena clean the kitchen. Once that was done, she said that she had errands to run in town, leaving me on my own, so I went into the living room and sat quietly on the sofa letting the case, cases, drift through my mind.

It's a form of active meditation, something I'd not being doing enough of since my arrival in Texas. In fact, that morning, I'd felt so crappy, I'd foregone my usual morning run, so, to make up for it, I decided to meditate.

I let everything I knew about the case just float around in my mind, making no effort to order or relate the disparate bits of information, instead, seeing them without consciously looking, to see what organic connections might form. It was like looking at a kaleidoscope, with the colors merging and separating at random, forming abstract patterns that never held together for long.

Here's what I knew.

Loren Caldwell undoubtedly worked for Global Energy, but for some reason, the company, or at least the company's security chief, was denying that relationship. Nancy Jo Billings, though, basically confirmed his Global employment with the fragment of a phone conversation she'd overheard.

Global Energy was facing financial problems, and probably in dire need of new sources of energy in order to survive in the dog-eat-dog world of the energy industry.

Caldwell was attempting to purchase at least five plots of land in the Poseyville area, worthless land for which he was willing, apparently, to pay significantly above market value.

GeoSync, the organization Caldwell claimed to work for did not, according to Heather's research, exist.

Bottom line: Caldwell was up to something, and that something had to do with the land. I was beginning to suspect either oil or natural gas deposits, the only two things that would be of interest to Global Energy.

Dudley Jarvis was intent on Winston *not* selling his land to Caldwell, to the extent of offering to better Caldwell's offer.

Jarvis was also prowling the disputed piece of real estate—I was convinced that the light I'd seen the night I went into the swamp, had been Jarvis with a flashlight.

Could it be that Caldwell hadn't offered to buy land from Jarvis, and he was jealous of Winston for receiving one? Was Jarvis aware of what Caldwell was up to?

Bottom line on this aspect of the case; Dudley Jarvis was also up to something. I was still convinced that he had some kind of illegal operation going in the swamp, but, whether or not it was related to what Caldwell was doing was a puzzle that I was determined to solve, and that would mean a visit to the Jarvis farm.

Just as I snapped out of my slight fugue, my phone rang. I felt the vibration against my chest a nanosecond before I heard the sound of the ring tone. I looked at the screen; it was Heather calling.

"Morning, Heather," I said. "What's new?"

"Hey, boss man, I got some more information." She sounded chipper. Whatever had been bothering her was apparently settled.

"Should I take notes?"

"Probably no need," she said. "It's not all that complicated."

"Okay, shoot."

"First, Global Energy and Loren Caldwell. The company's in dire straits. If they don't come up with some new energy supplies they might have to file for Chapter 11, or in a worst case scenario, Chapter 7."

Thanks to my long association with Quincy Chang, an old army buddy, and one of the senior partners in Holcombe, Stein and Chang, the law firm that has Heather and me on retainer, I knew that Chapter 11 was the law that covered bankruptcy for corporations that allowed them to restructure their debts and organization after suffering heavy losses. It's a common course of action for companies that overextend and find themselves unable to satisfy creditors. Chapter 7, on the other hand, was some serious shit. That involved the liquidation of the company. If Global Energy was even *thinking* about Chapter 7, they were really up the creek, and that could cause them to do some pretty desperate stuff, like pulling a scam to cheat people out of the honest value of their property.

"That might explain what Caldwell's up to here in Poseyville," I said. "By the way, yesterday, I met a dude named Alan Grayson who claims to be Global's head of security. See what you can—"

"Way ahead of you there. Alan Grayson *is* chief security officer for Global Energy, and he and Loren Caldwell are buddies; they served in the army together, and went to work for Global at the same time."

"Whoa, how'd you find this out?"

"I made a list of the executives of Global and was researching them when I ran across the page to an army engineer alumni web site when I was doing Caldwell. There was a photo from a reunion they had two months ago showing him and his old unit buddy, Alan Grayson, arms around each other's shoulders. When I did a little more digging on the two of them I found that they'd both been hired by Global right out of the army."

The pieces were beginning to fall into place. Grayson had blatantly lied to me about Caldwell. But the little tidbit Heather had unearthed did at least give me a bit of leverage to use when I next confronted Caldwell.

My first stop, though, was the Jarvis place. Like Caldwell, Dudley Jarvis had a little explaining to do.

* * *

The Jarvis house was similar to Winston's, but the yard in front was sorely in need of attention. Weeds grew in ragged clumps, crowding out a pathetic attempt at a lawn, and like Angus Murphy's place, rotting tires lay scattered about. I've never understood the tendency of some people to keep old tires and leave them around to collect water to become breeding grounds for mosquitos, especially in Texas and other parts of the Deep South, where mosquitos are almost as big as dragon flies. I also wondered, looking at the sorry state of his place, where Jarvis expected to get enough money to top Caldwell's offer on Winston's land; yet another piece of evidence pointing to something shady.

Just as I pulled my rental up behind Jarvis's pickup, he came around the side of the building with his shotgun over his right shoulder and a rusty iron bucket in his left hand. When he saw me, he stopped and watched through narrowed eyes as I got out of the vehicle.

"What do you want?" he asked in an unfriendly, demanding tone as I crossed the yard to him.

The mood was sure to become contentious eventually, but I didn't want it to start off that way. "I was hoping you had a few minutes," I said. "I'd like to pick your brain about a few things."

"Like what?"

I looked at the porch. He kept staring at me with a quizzical look on his face.

"Mind if we sit down?"

"You got that much to ask about? Why can't we just talk standing here?"

There was nothing friendly about this guy.

"Sure, if that's the way you want it," I said. "Has Loren Caldwell talked to you or your father about buying any of your land?"

At the word 'father' he flinched and frowned.

"No, he never did, why?"

"Well, I was just curious. You see, several other people have received offers. I was wondering why he'd want to buy the swampland on Winston's land, and not that part that's on your property as well."

"I couldn't tell you," he said. "I never talked to the man."

"Could he perhaps have talked to your father?"

His face darkened.

"No, he ain't talked to my daddy." His voice quavered as he spoke and his hands shook.

"Can you be sure of that? I mean, I know you work the farm, and I saw you the other day on the other side of your property. Maybe he came to the house when you were out, and your father sent him away and forgot to tell you about it."

"That ain't possible." He shook his head vehemently. "My father don't let anybody in the house when I'm out, he can't."

"Why is that?"

His grip on the shotgun was so tight, the knuckles on his sun-browned hand turned white.

"None of your fucking business, now I got nothing more to say to you, so get the hell off my property."

Charles Ray

Chapter 19

The young man knelt on the floor in front of the older man who sat hunched on a chair with his knees covered by a tattered blanket.

"Why, you old fool? Why did you have to do what you did? You ruined my life, you know that."

The old man, his rheumy blue eyes not really focused on anything, sat unmoving except for his right hand, like a misshapened claw, clenching and unclenching.

"That's right, you old shit, just sit there and stare at nothing. You ruined my life, and you don't give a shit, do you?"

He grabbed the old man by the front of his shirt and shook him, causing him to make mewling noises and dart his eyes from side to side.

"I ought to put you out of your misery, you old bastard," the young man said, spittle spewing out of his mouth and dotting the old man's face, to join the line of spittle that dribbled from his slack lips. "But, I'd rather let you sit here and suffer. I know you hear me, and you understand what I'm saying. One day, you're gonna die, and then you'll rot in hell for what you done. For now, though, I'll just keep waiting on you, and watching you suffer."

The mewling sound turned to more of a moan, and the old man's eyes rolled back in their sockets.

"That hurt? I hope it does. Yeah, I hope it hurts real bad."

With one last shake, he let the old man slump back into the chair. He stood and looked down at the wizened figure. There was, in his eyes, not even a glimmer of pity or compassion.

Then, he puffed out a breath and spun on his heel and left the room.

The old man continued to sit, staring off into space. The moaning changed back to a mewling sound, "Sah-ee, sah-ee." A line of tears seeped from the corner of his eyes and flowed across his craggy, sunken cheeks.

Chapter 20

After my unsatisfactory encounter with Dudley Jarvis, I decided to drive into Poseyville and have a little chat with Loren Caldwell.

It was that time of morning when your breakfast has already digested, but it's still too early for lunch. Despite that, my stomach was growling. Maybe being pissed off makes me hungry, I'm not sure, but I was sure that Dudley Jarvis was really pissing me off *and* I was feeling hungry. I didn't like his shitty attitude, and I really hated the fact that he presented a pisser of a puzzle and I couldn't seem to find the key that would lead to a solution.

I mulled that conundrum as I drove to town, and was still thinking about it when I pulled into the Bide a While parking lot and nosed into a parking space near the side entrance of the building that led to the conference room that Caldwell was renting.

My dark mood lifted as I got out of the car; when I saw the door open and Caldwell step out into the late-morning sunlight and start, head down, toward the silver BMW parked a few spaces away. He looked up, startled, as my shadow fell across him.

"Uh, Mr. Pennyback . . . nice seeing you again," he said, but the look in his eyes said that it was anything but nice. "I hope you're the bearer of good tidings. Has your cousin finally decided to accept my offer?"

"He's still thinking on it. There are a few things I need to clear up to help him make a decision. Do you have a few minutes to talk to me . . . privately?"

He looked hesitant. He didn't want to talk to me, but there was also a greedy look in his eyes, and as it usually does with people, greed won out.

"I was just going for an early lunch," he said. "If you'd like to join me, we can talk over a meal."

"Sounds fine," I said. "I'll follow you in my car."

We drove for about ten minutes, out to the main street, right, and then a left just before the turnoff to Winston's place, along a two-lane blacktop road lined on both sides by small farms and a few tin-roofed houses with small truck gardens behind them, until he pulled into a red clay field in the middle of which sat an unpretentious white building with a sign that read, 'Miss Kitty's Eats.'

The parking lot had three pickups and a rusty old Chevy Impala parked off to the side of the building. Caldwell parked his BMW near the front, and I pulled in beside him.

"I didn't know this place was here," I said when I got out.

"One of the locals told me about it," he said. "I'm from Iowa originally, and I've just never developed a taste for barbecue or having everything fried. This is the only place in this one-horse town where you can get a decent meat loaf and baked potatoes. I hope you don't mind."

I didn't really. Not that I have anything against fried food, and I'll drive a long way out of the way for good barbecue, but Sandra has for years tried to get me to eat healthier. Besides, meat loaf didn't sound half bad.

"No, I don't mind at all."

I followed him into the place.

It was shallow, looking more like a Pullman dining car than a regular building, with four booths seating four on each side of the front door along the front wall under the large windows, and a counter that covered about three-quarters of the back wall. There were twelve stools at the counter, four men dressed in faded and rumpled overalls sat on the stools at the left end of the counter. Other than looking up briefly, they paid us no attention. The cash register sat behind the counter at the center point, and behind the cash register sat a demure looking middle-aged lady with a large, and I mean a *large* blonde hairdo, that looked like it took a can of hair spray to hold it in place. She had round, rosy cheeks and dark brown eyes, and beneath the blue blouse she wore, that was open at the neck, were two *large* breasts that threatened to burst through the v-shaped opening. She looked up and beamed a thousand-watt smile when Caldwell entered.

"Hey there, hon, y'all eatin' lunch early today," she said in a reedy voice. "You havin' your usual?"

"That I am, Miss Kitty," Caldwell said. "Not sure what my friend here is having."

"How 'bout you, hon, what you havin'?"

"What's his usual?" I asked.

"He always orders the meat loaf, baked potato with sour cream, kale, and corn muffins for his main course, and blackberry pie with vanilla ice cream for dessert. His drink is unsweetened iced tea."

The only thing that sounded wrong with that meal was the number of total calories it probably contained. Otherwise, my stomach was tapping out a 'go ahead' signal against my belt buckle.

"Make that two of his usual," I said. "And, could I get a slice of lemon in my tea?"

"Sure can, hon. Y'all go on and take a seat wherever you're comfortable, and I'll have your food out directly."

That turned out to be the last booth on the right, which was fine with me, except that it was near the men's room. I assumed that the lady's room was near the end booth at the other side, and frankly would have preferred it because, as much as I hate to admit it, women's toilets are just nicer smelling than the can for guys. Of course, that would've meant sitting right under the four guys at the counter, and I had a feeling that Caldwell wanted privacy.

"Go ahead and take a seat," he said. "I have to go drain the pipe."

My luck was still running good. That enabled me to take the side of the booth with the wall to my back and giving me a view of the entrance and the whole interior—my preferred seating, especially in a new location. Miss Kitty brought our tea while he was away, and I was a quarter done with mine by the time he came back, which coincided with her bringing out two trays containing our main course.

As he took his seat opposite me, she put our food on the table, went away and came back with little white bowls of sour cream, bacon bits and chopped onions, and a saucer of butter pats which she put in the center of the table.

"For your baked potatoes and bread. Enjoy," she said, and went back behind the counter.

I sliced open my baked potato and spooned a generous amount of sour cream, onions, and bacon bits and then sprinkled a bit of salt and a generous amount of black pepper on top of that. Bottles of Tabasco and catchup, and a small carafe of vinegar were already on the table. I put Tabasco and catchup on my meat loaf and vinegar on the kale.

While I was buttering my corn muffin, Caldwell was busy using his knife to make sure no food item on his plate touched any other food item.

As I ate I watched him, fascinated at the way he fastidiously arranged things. First, he used the knife to shape the meatloaf into a wedge shape, and then he scraped the kale into a small pile and pushed it around until there was a knife-blade's width between it and the meat. He couldn't shape the baked potato or corn muffin, so he shoved them around until each also had its area of white space around it. The guy talked like an escapee from a 50s era TV show, and had some real issues; not exactly what I would have expected of a con artist.

I was enjoying the rich, smoky taste of the meat, the tartness of the vinegar-laden greens, and alternately, the sweetness of the corn muffin and the rich taste of the baked potato. Caldwell, on the other hand started at the portion of food nearest him, and ate his way around the plate counterclockwise, chewing each forkful twenty times, and swallowing before moving on to the next. As he reached the first portion, he would take a small sip of iced tea, and start all over again.

This was not a person who chatted while he ate, an art that my best friend, DC Metro Police Detective Buster Mayweather has perfected. As he ate, Caldwell's brow was furrowed in concentration as if he was worried that while chewing he would lose his place. I was so distracted watching his little ritual I almost stabbed myself in the cheek with a forkful of meat loaf. Caldwell didn't notice.

When my plate was empty and he had just small amounts of everything left—the corn muffin had been reduced to the same size as the small mounds of meat loaf and kale, and the remaining innards of the baked potato had been scooped into a similar sized mound inside the peel, which he'd been careful *not* to eat. My tea glass was empty. His had about half an inch left. He wiped his lips with the napkin, adjusted the glass until it was a hand's width from the plate, which was two finger widths from the edge of the table, and then placed the fork and knife crossed on the plate, careful not to touch the uneaten food. He then sat back and looked at me.

"Well, Al, do you mind if I call you Al?" I shook my head. "Well, Al, while we wait for dessert, what is it you wish to talk about?"

I lifted my empty tea glass to catch Miss Kitty's attention and waggled it to show I wanted a refill. She smiled and nodded. That done, I put the glass to the side and braced my elbows on the edge of the table, and propped my chin on my overlapped fingers.

"I'd like to know first, why you *really* want to buy that property."

"I told you—"

"I know what you told me," I said, cutting him off with a sharp look. "But, you and I both know it's not the truth, so why don't you come clean and tell me what it is you really want."

"Really, it's just for science. This place was once under a great inland sea. Exploring the sediment could tell us a lot about what life on earth was like in that era."

It sounded like he'd memorized a brochure—and it sounded like total bullshit.

"Right, and you're willing to put out major money to get that knowledge, right?"

"Of course we are. Besides, one hundred thousand's not all that much money."

"What about the hundred grand you're offering to each of the four or five others? Half a million or so starts to sound like real money to me."

His eyebrows twitched. I had to give the guy credit, though, other than that, he didn't react.

"We need to research several sites to ensure the integrity of our data."

And, he was pretty quick on his feet.

"Where do you get your money?"

"GeoSync is funded by private donors."

"So, you get no government money?"

"Right. Government has too many requirements and restrictions. This way, we're free to research what and how we wish."

"I guess that explains why I can find no record of the existence of GeoSync."

"Maybe you just didn't look in the right place."

"Yeah, maybe," I said. "What do you know about Global Energy?"

The eyebrows twitched again; a little more this time.

"I . . . once worked for Global Energy, but I quit to work for GeoSync."

"When was that?"

"Uh . . . six months ago."

Bingo. I had him in a lie; well, I had him in a bunch of lies, but this one I had information to hang him with.

"When's the last time you talked to your friend, Alan Grayson?"

Now, a shifting of the eyes to the right and back accompanied the brow twitch.

"Alan . . . Grayson? Why would you ask that?"

"You and Grayson are friends, right?"

The guy was cool, except for the eye twitches, but he must have sensed that something wasn't quite right, and no matter how well trained you are, sometimes your body will just give you away when you're backed into a corner. In his case it was the little beads of sweat above his upper lip that did it.

"Yes, we are. Why?"

"Just curious. When was the last time you spoke to him?"

He hesitated. The average person might not have noticed it, but I'm not the average person. The army trained me to conduct interrogations as well as resist them. I know most of the things to look for, and the speed at which people answer questions is one of them. A hesitation, even a slight one, an intake of breath, or sudden small movement of a body part after a question, indicates a couple of things; the person is about to lie, or is considering whether or not to tell the truth.

"Not too long ago," he said finally. "A couple months, I think. We were at a reunion of our old army unit. We had a few drinks and shot the shit about old times. Why do you want to know that, and what does my being friends with Alan have to do with anything?"

The first true thing he'd said, and now the sweat was beaded on his brow.

"You two started working at Global Energy at the same time, right?"

"Yeah, we got out of the army around the same time. Alan actually started working for Global a week before I did. He recommended I apply, I did, and they hired me."

"While there, you saw each other a lot?"

"Now and again. I worked in field operations, while Alan was in the security division, so we were often in different towns."

"He must be pretty good," I said. "To now be head of security."

Brow twitch, eye flick, and a couple of blinks.

"You seem to know a lot about me. What are you, some kind of cop?"

"No, I'm not a cop."

Literally true. The cops I know, including Buster, do *not* think of private investigators as part of the law enforcement community; any more than they think of private security guards, armed or not, as real cops. The fact that I've often solved crimes that the cops had stumbled over—read, screwed up—notwithstanding, I am not a cop. I could tell from the way his eyes narrowed, though, that he wasn't totally buying my answer; another sign that he was up to no good. That's the problem with being on the wrong side of the law, you're constantly looking over your shoulder, literally and metaphorically, and because you *are* up to no good, there's a tendency to suspect everyone else of being up to no good.

"Well, you certainly ask questions like one."

"Have you had a lot of experience being questioned by the police?"

"No, of course not."

"Then, how do you know I ask questions like one?"

"I watch TV."

Of course. Everyone watches a few episodes of cop shows on TV and they're experts. I could have told him that, but it would only have validated his suspicion, so I decided to go with a non-answer.

"Trust me, real life's a lot different than what you see on TV."

"Even if I never watched TV, you still ask a lot of questions that I don't normally get from people when I try to buy their land. Why are you so curious?"

"I'm the curious type."

"How is this helping you decide if your cousin should sell me his land or not?"

"Let's just say I'd like to know that he's dealing with an honest person."

He smiled and steepled his hands, staring at me over the tips of his fingers. "Well, I can assure you that I'm being perfectly straight, and I'm offering your cousin a great deal," he said. "So, are you going to convince him to accept my offer?"

Just then, Miss Kitty brought our dessert. The sweet, rich smell of blackberries preceded her by several feet. His head whipped around.

"Y'all ready for dessert?" the big haired woman asked, as she put a plate in front of each of us.

I looked from her to the large slice of pie with a baseball-sized lump of vanilla ice cream on it to Caldwell, who was already arranging his plate so the narrow part of the pie wedge was to his left. He then took his knife and fork and began slicing the pie from the narrow end to the wide end, measuring to make each slice the thickness of two fork tines. If this guy was married, I pitied his wife, or anyone else who had to sit at a table with him more than once. He was, though, totally preoccupied with his pie, so I decided to work on my own and pick up the conversation after we finished eating.

The pie was good, there was no doubt, and when Miss Kitty asked if we'd like an after lunch coffee, I decided to hell with it and agreed; black, no sugar, please. Caldwell asked for two teaspoons of sugar and one tablespoon of half and half, no milk for him. Miss Kitty looked at me and rolled her eyes. Caldwell didn't seem to notice.

"Now, where we? Oh, yes, are you going to tell your cousin to sell?"

"I don't think so."

His face went tense, and his gaze bore into me.

"Why not?"

How much should I tell him at this point? I knew he was lying to me. I knew that he still worked for Global Energy. But, so far, I couldn't prove any of it. He was offering over market value for the land, which was, on the one hand a plus in his column, but if he was willing to offer that much it had to mean the value of the property was significantly greater. The energy industry is not known for its generosity. From the days of the wildcat oilmen, these guys were only interested in how much money they could make. Their goal wasn't a fair return on investment, but maximum profits. I just needed to find out what his game was.

"I just have a feeling you're not telling my cousin . . . or me the whole story."

He looked at me through narrow slits.

"What are you, really?" he asked. "Are you some kind of investigator with the FTC, or the FBI?"

"No," I answered honestly. "I'm not a federal investigator."

"Damn if you're not starting to sound like one. You say you're Mr. Jones's cousin, but you don't talk like a local. Where are you from?"

"I am his cousin. I don't have a local accent because I left Texas as a teenager and joined the army. I sort of grew up all over the world."

I hoped he wouldn't notice that I hadn't answered his question fully. Telling him that I was from the DC area would undercut my denial of being a fed. The way he was looking at me, and the tic in his cheek muscles said he feared I might be with the government, and it made him nervous. Another piece of information that convinced me that he was up to something shady. If only I could figure out how to use it to my advantage.

"You think I'm trying to cheat your cousin?"

"Cheat's a strong word," I said. "I don't know that I'd go that far. But, put yourself in my place. Wouldn't you be suspicious if someone offered to pay top dollar for what looks like a worthless piece of land?"

"No, I wouldn't be suspicious. I'd be happy to be able to get something out of land that would otherwise just sit there without making me a penny."

"Well, there's also the problem I have with a research organization that you say is not connected with the deep pockets of the government, being able to offer the money you're offering for that worthless land."

He smiled. A tight-lipped, vulpine smile that was totally without mirth. "You obviously don't know much about research organizations." He was right about that. "The government *does* have deep pockets, but it also has reams of regulations and restrictions. Government funding for research mainly goes to projects that have some kind of military application. We're doing pure research, and we just happen to be lucky enough to have some wealthy people who are willing to fund it. You might not be aware of this, but some wealthy people like to put all that money they're sitting on to some worthwhile purpose."

Damn if he didn't sound credible. This guy could have been a successful carnival barker or used car salesman. But, I wasn't buying what he was selling.

"It would help if you could give me some literature about your organization," I said. "Or, even better, if you could point me to some place where I could learn more about you and what you do."

That caused his brow to wrinkle, and his lips were clenched so tight they turned almost white. It took him a few seconds to come up with a response; another sign of deception.

"That will take some time," he said. "I don't carry such things around with me."

"That's okay. All I have is time." I gave him my mobile number. "Call me when you have the information. Once I've had a chance to look it over, I'll let you know whether or not I'll advise my cousin to sell."

"Don't take too long. There are other people here who *are* willing to sell. I just might talk to your cousin's neighbor after all. I'd hate to see him lose out on this opportunity."

"If you're talking about Dudley Jarvis, you might as well save your time. He's already tried to talk my cousin out of selling. It seems he doesn't want any of the land out there changing hands."

Now, he was looking angry. He made an effort to control it, but the tightening of his jaw muscles and the creases radiating out from the corners of his eyes gave it away.

"We'll see what he says when he hears how much I'm willing to pay. I only have so much patience, Mr. Pennyback, and you've just about used it up."

"Good luck with that," I said. "As to exhausting your patience, I have that effect on people." I stood and started toward Miss Kitty at the cash register.

"Never mind," he said. "Lunch is on me. It'll be the only thing you and your family get from me if you don't convince your cousin to sell that land."

He stood, straightened the creases out of his jacket and strutted to the cash register with me in his wake. I do think he just issued a threat. But, from a guy who sorted his food before eating it, I found it hard to take it seriously.

"How was your lunch, hon?" Miss Kitty asked.

"It was fine, Miss Kitty," Caldwell said stiffly. "I'm paying for both of us. How much do I owe you?"

She pulled an order sheet from a stack beside the register, and held it up close to her face. "Two lunch specials, that'll be nineteen-sixty."

He pulled out his wallet and extracted a twenty and a five and laid them on the counter. "Keep the change," he said. He turned to me. "Remember what I said, Mr. Pennyback. My offer to your cousin's only open for another twenty-four hours. After that, he gets nothing."

He spun on his heels and strode out.

Miss Kitty chuckled. "He's a bit high-strung, that one."

"I think I upset him."

"Aw, hon, don't you fret none about it," she said. "He always seems like he just sucked on a lemon, and I swear if he don't have the oddest eatin' habits I ever seen. But, he tips well."

"Yeah, he is strange, but he did pay for my lunch, so I guess I can't complain. By the way, the food was great."

"Well, y'all tell your friends, and come on back anytime, you hear."

Chapter 21

Caldwell's BMW wasn't in the lot when I exited. I must have really pissed him off. I debated driving back to his office to take another run at him, but then decided to wait until I got more information from Heather, so I drove back to Winston's instead.

Winston was still doing chores, and Rowena was busy in the kitchen and not being her usual flirtatious self. I went to my room and sat on the edge of the bed near the nightstand and tried to make sense of things.

That didn't do me any good. I sat there with my notebook open on the nightstand and my pen in hand, and nothing new came to me. I even tried meditating, but it didn't help. I knew that Loren Caldwell was pulling some kind of con, probably on behalf of Global Energy, but didn't have a shred of proof. Short of kidnapping him and coercing a confession, it was beginning to look like I never would get any either. Then, there was the conundrum of Dudley Jarvis. The dude was fixated on Winston's piece of swamp land, and it made no sense. I was going to have to check the place out in daylight, which meant that I'd probably confront him and his shotgun. If I'd been anyplace other than Texas, I would've concluded that the chance of him taking a shot at me was minimal. But, this *was* Texas, the land where people love guns and football, probably in that order. I would have to be real careful when I went—and, I'd decided that I would go—and try to see him before he saw me.

So, of my two cases, the one that was most important was up in the air unless Heather came up with something, leaving me to take care of the one closer to home, which was more of a puzzle than a case, but it was a nuisance that I was confident I could take care of.

I'd just given up trying to get anything done and lay back on the bed when Rowena yelled up the stairs for me to get my tail down for supper.

Supper was a subdued affair. Rowena had made tuna salad and toasted wheat bread. Winston started to complain, but she shushed him by reminding him that he'd promised to do at least one meal a week without meat. He shut up, but glowered at her for the entire meal. It was actually pretty good, and the unsweetened iced tea went well with it. After supper, I helped her with the dishes, while Winston grabbed a bottle of Lone Star beer and went to the front porch.

Dishes finished, Rowena and I grabbed four beers each and joined him.

He raised his bottle. "I reckon next you gon' be tellin' me I can't have myself a little taste every night," he said to Rowena. Then, he turned to me. "This gal go off to college and come back here fulla all these hifalutin' ideas and such. It's enough to drive a man to drink."

"Which would be a short trip, daddy," Rowena shot back. "Since you already drink like a fish."

"I do not. 'Sides, fish don't drink. If they did, all the water'd soon be dried up."

"Yes, you do, and that was just a figure of speech meaning you drink to excess."

He looked at me with a stricken expression on his face. "You see what I got to put up with. Girl done changed so much I ain't got no idea what she talkin' 'bout half the time."

"Well, she did teach you how to use a computer," I said. I didn't want to take sides, and I didn't like being caught in the middle of what sounded like a long-running conversation.

"Yeah, she done that," he said. "I just wish she'd quit talkin' so snitty. Sometime I think she done forgot where she come from."

Rowena laughed. Hers wasn't a ladylike laugh, but from deep down in her gut. You have to appreciate a woman who is not afraid to laugh like that.

"Okay, daddy," she said. "I'll cut you some slack tonight. Tell us, Cousin Al, what have you found out about this Caldwell guy? Is it a square deal?"

"I can't say yet. There is definitely something fishy about Caldwell, but I don't have conclusive proof . . . yet."

"Wow, you sound just like one of those detectives on TV."

"That's 'cause he is one," Winston said.

Her eyes went round as small saucers and she clapped a hand over her mouth. "No joking? You're like one of those private detectives?"

"Guilty as charged," I said.

"That's why I ast him to come down and help me," Winston said. "He's real famous up there in Washington, DC. The newspapers up there call him the Brown Knight."

Rowena sat there looking at me all goggle-eyed with her mouth hanging open.

"Wow! Can I see your gun?"

"I don't carry a weapon," I said. "I don't even own one."

"I thought all detectives had a . . . what do they call them on TV . . . a piece."

"Yes, that's what they call them, but it's only on TV that private investigators run around with weapons. Mostly what we do is watch people and read papers. A lot like what I'm doing now. Sometimes I have to find people and deliver papers. It's not nearly as sexy as they make it look on TV."

"What do you do when a bad guy comes after you?"

"If I can't beat him off with my feet or fists, I run like hell."

She shook her head. "You're joking, right?"

"No, I'm not joking. My partner and I use our brains to solve cases. There's seldom any violence. On occasion, yes, but like I said, if I can't beat 'em, I beat feet."

"Speaking of Heather, did she find out anything more?" Winston asked.

"Who's Heather?" Rowena asked.

I explained how my company was organized and the roles that Heather and I played respectively.

"Wow!" she said when I'd finished. She was saying 'wow' a lot. "You have a female partner who is a whiz with computers. So, you're really into the high-tech stuff."

"Heather's the tech genius. I just do the grunt work."

"Speaking of which, what have you found out so far?"

"Not a lot." I took a long swallow of beer. Lone Star beer is bitter and acidic, but cold, it's not bad, especially after the first two or three sips. "I'm pretty sure that Caldwell's working for Global Energy, and I think he and Global's security chief are working some kind of land grab scam. They're not very good at it, though. They didn't even coordinate their stories." I explained the differences between their stories about when Caldwell left the company. "Of course, that by itself is not enough to prove anything."

"What do you need to prove it?"

"Well, if I could somehow show them communicating, either meeting up or talking on the phone, that would give me leverage to hammer Caldwell. Grayson, that's the security guy, is impossible to get to with all the security they have up there in Lufkin."

Rowena was now looking at me with a dreamy look in her eyes. I get that sometimes. People have this fanciful notion of what a private detective does, and they get all gooey. If they only knew. When I'm not chasing down deadbeat clients on behalf of Holcombe, Stein and Chang, I'm following some character to prove he's not as injured as he claims so the insurance company, that also happens to be a client of the law firm that retains me, doesn't have to pay out a bundle of money. Heather, my partner, is usually stuck at her computer, ferreting out information. Rarely do we get involved with the sexy stuff like you see on TV, with people with guns taking shots at us, and when we do, I can assure you it's not sexy.

"So," she said. "How are you going to get the goods on Caldwell? Will you snatch him and take him somewhere and give him the third degree?"

"No, Rowena, I will not snatch him. Kidnapping's a crime, and even as a private investigator, because I'm on retainer by a law firm, I'm an officer of the court of sorts, sworn to uphold the law. I also do *not* give people the third degree. Coercive methods of interrogation don't usually yield much useful information anyway."

Her expression changed to one of disappointment.

"Do you do *any* of the things they do on TV?"

"Not even one of them."

"That sounds boring."

I pointed my index finger at her. "Now you got it. That's what working as a PI is like most of the time, just boring routine."

Winston laughed.

"Now, girl, will you hush up and let Al tell us what he *can* do?"

"Well, Winston, at this point, I'm not sure. I'm thinking of watching Caldwell in the hopes he'll slip up and give me a clue as to what he's really up to. In the meantime,

Heather's trying to verify that he's still employed by Global Energy. Beyond that . . . I just don't know."

He reached over with his hand the size of a small catcher's mitt and patted me on the knee. "Don't you worry, Al. I know you gon' come up with something."

The phone in the living room rang. We looked at each other. The phone rang again.

Rowena made a huffing noise. "Oh, I'll get it." She heaved herself from her chair and padded into the living room.

The phone rang two more times before she answered. I could hear her mumbling, but couldn't make out what she was saying.

A few minutes later she came back out to the porch.

"Al, there's some woman named Nancy Jo on the phone saying she's got to talk to you," she said. "She sounds really upset."

Rowena looked at me with raised brows and deep suspicion in her eyes.

"She's Caldwell's secretary," I said, rising and heading for the living room. "She's another possibility for getting the goods on him. I'll see what she wants."

She still looked skeptical as I squeezed past her.

When I picked up the phone, I could hear ragged breathing.

"Nancy Jo, Al Pennyback here. What's the matter?"

"Oh, Al, I need to see you . . . it's urgent . . . you could be in danger."

"Whoa, what kind of danger?"

"I don't want to go into it on the phone, could you come here?"

There was no doubt she was upset, even fearful.

"Okay, you hang tight," I said. "I'll be there in a few minutes."

Chapter 22

I pulled up outside Nancy Jo Billings' farm house fifteen minutes later, having broken almost everyone of Poseyville's speed limits to get there.

I parked directly in front of her door, and shut the engine off. As I was getting out of the car I noticed the curtain beside the door move, and then the light above the door came on.

The door opened as I approached it. She was standing there, backlit by a lamp in the living room. The thigh-length bathrobe she wore was so thin I could see the outline of her body through it. Her hair, limp and clinging to her skull, was shining from moisture. When I stepped through the door, she grabbed my arm and pulled me in, quickly closing the door.

I turned, and she threw herself against my body, and wrapped her arms around me. I could feel the heat of her body through the thin robe, and from the way her generous breasts mashed against my chest I could tell she wasn't wearing a bra.

"I'm so glad you got here okay," she murmured against my chest. "I was worried they might have gone after you already."

I grasped her shoulders and gently pushed her away and looked down at her. Even with the worry frown on her face, without the makeup and oversized hairdo, she was an attractive woman. But, even if I'd been interested, her words triggered alarms in my brain.

"Who might be after me?"

"Mr. Caldwell and whoever he called."

I pushed her gently toward the couch. "Let's sit down," I said. "And tell me what you're talking about."

She sat down and patted the adjacent cushion. I sat on the easy chair to her right, which caused her to frown.

"You don't want to sit next to me? Don't you find me attractive?"

"I think you're one hell of a beautiful woman, Nancy Jo, but right now we need to focus on something else. Now, do you want to tell me why you called me?"

"Would you like a drink, Al . . . may I call you Al? I could use one right now."

Her lame attempt at flirting with me was further weakened by the fear that was as plain on her face as McDonalds' arches on a dark night. But, if I was going to get anything out of her, I would have to play along . . . to a point.

"Sure, I could use a drink. What are you having?"

"You know I like tequila."

"Tequila it is, then."

When she stood, the robe parted just enough for me to see that she wasn't wearing panties either. I began to wonder if she *really* had something important to tell me, or if this was just a clumsy attempt at seduction, but I bit back the snarky remark that was forming in my mind. She did look worried, and I needed to know why.

She went to the credenza and took out the bottle of tequila and two glasses.

"You want lime and salt with it?" she asked.

"Why don't we do it neat? That salt and lime routine's just for tourists. In the small villages they don't do it."

"Have you been to any small Mexican villages?"

"A few."

She looked quizzically at me, but when I didn't speak, she shrugged and came back to the couch. Seated demurely, or as demurely as possible with so much leg showing, she filled both glasses to near the brims and handed me one.

"Do we chug-a-lug it, or sip it?"

"Neither," I said. "We take healthy swigs and swallow it quickly." To demonstrate, I lowered the level in my glass about half an inch. It felt like molten lava going down my throat, but I kept my expression impassive.

She copied me, except for the expression. She looked like she was swallowing broken glass.

"Whew! That's some potent stuff."

"You want to take it easy and pace yourself. It can sneak up on you. Now, while we're still sober enough to form words, you want to tell me why you called?"

She put her glass on the coffee table and turned to face me, showing even more thigh, and allowing the top of the robe to swing open, showing the generous curves of her breasts.

"Mr. Caldwell came back to the office real late today," she said. "And, he was royally pissed. When I asked him what was bothering me, he snapped at me to mind my own fucking business and barricaded himself in his office."

"I had lunch with him today, and we finished early, so he must have gone somewhere else after leaving the restaurant. I think I might have pissed him off."

"Yeah, that's what I'm getting to." She crossed her legs, treating me to a sight that made it hard to concentrate. "Soon as he got in his office, he was on the phone, and he was shouting so loud, I could almost hear what he was saying sitting at my desk."

"Almost?"

"Hey, he was mean to me, and it pissed *me* off. I don't care what kind of day he had; he had no right to talk to me like that. Anyway, I tip-toed over to the door and listened to what he was saying. Those portable walls they use at the hotel are as thin as cardboard. I could hear his end of the conversation as clear as if I was in the room with him."

"And, you heard him talking about me?"

"Not at first. He was talking to some guy named Alan. He said the deals he'd already made fell through. Seems the landowners decided they wanted to wait a while. Some old codger, those are his words not mine, some old codger named Angus Murphy got to the others and convinced them to wait a bit before signing the papers. He was silent for a while after he said that, so I figure this Alan was talking, but then he started shouting again, and that's when he mentioned you."

"What did he say about me?"

"He said you were the one who got to Murphy, and poisoned him against the deal, and that you were a real pain in the ass who would have to be dealt with. Then he said not to worry, though, because he was going to take care of you and get you out of Global Energy's hair for good. That's when I got plumb scared. The way he said it, he sounded so mean, like maybe he plans to kill you or something."

While I couldn't totally rule that out, I didn't think Loren Caldwell was the type to try something like that himself. He didn't even impress me as the type who would hire someone to kill me either—of course, that was mainly wishful thinking on my part. When it comes to money, people will do the strangest things. It just meant I'd have to watch my back a bit more carefully.

"He wouldn't be the first person who wanted me dead," I said. "But, I'm still here as you can see."

Her eyes went wide. "What are you? Most people, if someone said somebody was out to kill them would freak out. You take it like I'd just told you the time."

"Oh, I take it seriously, but there's no sense in losing your cool over it. My next step is to figure out how to turn Mr. Caldwell's little scam against him."

"Won't that be dangerous? This kinda proves he's working with Global Energy, and oil companies got a lot of money behind 'em. They won't be easy to beat. Are you going to the authorities?"

"No, not yet," I said. "Like you said, the company has a lot of money, and money equals clout. Right now, I don't have any evidence that would stand up in court, so I'll have to approach it in another way."

The information she'd provided wouldn't stand up in court, and exposing it would expose her, which I wasn't prepared to do. But, like the old folks always used to say, 'there's more than one way to skin a cat.' From what she'd overheard, Caldwell was under pressure to deliver the plots of land in Poseyville, and Angus Murphy's decision to convince his fellow landowners to join him in delaying the transfer—thanks to my meddling—a monkey wrench had been thrown into his plans. People who haven't been trained to operate under conditions of extreme stress, and that's the vast majority of people, make mistakes when they have to act under pressure. Caldwell had already made one mistake. Getting into a heated phone conversation and allowing his secretary to overhear was a rookie mistake. Now, what I had to do was increase the pressure a bit, and maybe, just maybe, I could push him into making a big enough mistake that it would allow me to topple his house of cards.

I stood, leaving my unfinished tequila on the coffee table.

"W-where are you going?" she asked.

"I have a lot to do tomorrow," I said. "Look, you might consider calling in sick tomorrow, just in case Caldwell is planning on something violent. I wouldn't want you to get caught in the crossfire."

"I d-don't know if I want to be here all alone." She stood and wrapped her arms around her chest, causing her breasts to bulge even more, threatening to pop right out of her robe. "What if he figures out I've been talking to you, and comes here?"

"Don't worry. I plan to keep him busy tomorrow, too busy to be even thinking about you. This is the safest place for you, trust me."

She walked around the coffee table and stood in front of me, close enough that I could feel the heat of her body.

"I don't know why, but I do trust you." She placed her palms against my chest. "You're a strange man, not at all like the men I'm used to. It's too bad you're already taken."

"Yeah, I suppose it is. Look, like I said before, it I wasn't already in a relationship, I'd be all over you like a bee in a flower garden. But, I'm not into one-night stands."

"A man of honor," she said huskily. "Not too many around anymore. Would you think you were cheating if I stole one little kiss?"

"That might not be such a good idea. Who knows where that might lead?"

She leaned in until her breasts were massaging my chest. I reacted as any man would react, but I kept my hands at my side.

"Oh, I think you have enough self-control for the both of us. Just one little old kiss?"

I can do this, I thought to myself. No you can't, a little voice in my head said. That was me, too. I was having a damned argument with myself, and I think I was losing.

"Okay, just one kiss, and nothing more."

She reached up with her right hand and grasped the back of my neck, pulling my head forward and down. At the same time, she pushed the full length of her body against mine. Her lips brushed against mine, as soft as the touch of a butterfly's wings. Her tongue poked against my lips and she pulled harder on my neck. I relaxed my lips and her tongue slipped inside my mouth. Hot and wet, it met and merged with my tongue. She tasted like tequila and something sweet. Her body moved against mine. I could feel every bump and indentation, and when I grasped her waist, all I felt under the thin fabric was her smooth, hot flesh. She moaned softly, the sound jerking me back to reality.

I gently disengaged, giving her a gentle pat on the fanny as I pulled away from her. She looked up at me with a dreamy expression. Her breasts strained against the robe as they rose and fell.

"Now, *that's* what I call a kiss," she said. "Did you like it?"

I nodded, not trusting myself to speak. Damn right I liked it. My body felt as tight as a tightly-wound guitar string. The physical reaction she'd caused made my pants feel uncomfortable in the crotch area.

I liked it a lot. But, I felt as guilty as hell.

Chapter 23

The drive back to Winston's place allowed me to calm down. Winston and Rowena were asleep. To avoid waking them, I brushed my teeth, splashed cold water on my face, and crawled into bed in my shorts and tee shirt.

Whether it was the tequila or the fact that I'd been going all day long, I fell asleep almost immediately. No drowsy period and slow drifting into slumber, more like stepping off a ledge into darkness. A long, quick fall into . . . nothingness.

The dream started very soon after I fell asleep.

* * *

It was, at first, like many of my past dreams. I was walking through a swirling mist. The surface beneath my feet, which I couldn't see, was spongy, giving with every step. My feet were moving, but, with the opaque white mist whirling around my head I felt no sensation of moving. It was if I was walking in place.

When the dreams first started, a few months after the death of my wife, Sara, and my six-year-old son, Ethan, in a senseless and totally avoidable accident, the mist, the sensation of pacing in place, scared the crap out of me, and I'd often wake up in a cold sweat and gasping for air. That was because at first that's all it was, me in this white fog. Then, gradually, the dreams changed. About two months into them, Sara and Ethan began to appear.

They were always on the other side of this little stream, standing in a peaceful woody glade. I could never get to them, never touch them, but I could talk to them. And, I could hear them, well, mostly Sara. Ethan, even as a spirit, was a shy kid who never talked much. He'd just stand there, huddled against his mother's leg smiling at me.

The dreams came regularly at first, usually when I'd been under stress, such as working a case that had hit a dead end. Sara and I would talk, and during that talk she would point me in the right direction.

I have to say here, for the record, I'm not really a superstitious person. I don't believe in ghosts, and once I woke up I knew that I'd been dreaming; that my subconscious mind was just working out my problems during my sleep, and it used a familiar medium to do it. Often we know things, but our conscious minds don't see the relevance or importance of what we know. It's then that our subconscious, through dreams, shunts us onto the right track.

The dreams hadn't come often over the past five years or so, about once every six months. So, this situation involving my cousin was triggering one. If Sandra had been with me, I would've probably discussed the case with her, and definitely would have talked with Heather about, and even probably Buster, Quincy, or Carlton 'Blood' Raine, my octogenarian retired-CIA friend.
They weren't around to serve as sounding boards, so my mind was defaulting back to its old routine.

But, this time, the dream was different. The only familiar element was the white mist. Usually, there'd be music, or the soft sound of wind or flowing water just before Sara appeared. There was no music, and the sounds I heard were like someone off in the distance moaning in pain.

As I strained to see ahead of me, I noticed something that caused the breath to get caught in my throat. The mist wasn't white after all. It was a dirty, dingy gray, with a grayish-red blob floating in the distance at about eye level.

The moans sent chills down my spine. That, too, was new. I'd never *felt* anything before except the soft caress of the wind on my face. Along with the chills, I could feel my heart pounding in my chest, and the throbbing of the veins in my neck.

The situation was so not copacetic, but once the dream started I pretty much had to go along for the ride until the end. I suppose I should've been able to wake myself up, but just as I'm a sucker for puzzles when I'm awake, my natural curiosity forces me to follow the trail of bread crumbs until I reach the witch's house.

The blob, now more red than gray, was getting larger, spreading out to the sides for several yards, and the moaning was getting louder.

I finally came to the edge of the stream. But, this time, it wasn't a crystal clear stream winding through a rich verdant landscape. The sluggish liquid that seemed to be moving in slow motion was dark red, almost black, just like the blood that pools under an eviscerated corpse. On the opposite bank of this river of . . . blood, instead of a lush, green copse of woods, the ground was as gray and cracked with jagged gray tree trunks thrusting upwards.

Except for the brief excursion to Winston's swamp, it'd been a long time since I'd done an operation in marsh land, but the scene before me was familiar for some reason. The thing about my dreams, though, is that I didn't seem to have full control of my thinking like I did when I was awake. My thoughts went where the dream led me.

I stood there, waiting. For a long time nothing happened except the moaning.

Then, I heard her voice. The sweet, dulcet tones of Sara's voice cut through the moans and eased the tension I'd been feeling.

"Hello, my love," she said.

"Hello, Sara," I responded. "Where are you? Why can't I see you?" This part of the dream still freaked me out a little. My lips weren't moving—at least, I couldn't tell if they were moving—nor did hers. I could hear her voice and mine clearly in my head. This time, though, her voice was muffled as if she was on the other side of a wall.

"It's not important, dearest. Just listen. There is a barrier between us, one that only my voice can penetrate."

"What kind of barrier?"

"I don't know. I can't see it, but I can feel it. It is . . . pain, oh, so much pain . . . and loneliness. They are so lonely."

"Who? Who is lonely?"

"I don't know," her voice echoed in my mind. "There are so very many voices. They're crying out for someone to bring them peace. They want someone to know what happened to them. They want justice."

I paused, my gaze drawn to the slow-flowing red liquid. Then, I felt a coldness flowing over my entire body, like icy hands pawing at me.

"I don't understand, Sara," I said. "Can you try to reach out to them? Tell me who they are, and why they want . . . justice?"

"I can't, my love. I am prevented from coming any closer. I can hear you, but I'm not allowed to see you. The voices are saying that they must have justice first."

What the hell did that mean? Who were they, and why were they putting themselves between Sara and me? I wanted to shout at them, demand that they show themselves, but I couldn't form the words. I opened my mouth, but no sound came out. The moaning grew louder in my ears, so loud that I could no longer hear Sara.

Then, I began to hear words mixed in with the moaning. *"Find us. Set us free. Help us, please."*

The darkness across the stream deepened, becoming a roiling black cloud tinged with red. I felt cold.

* * *

I woke up, tangled in the sheet, my body slick with sweat. I was breathing hard, as hard as if I'd just run a cross-country four miles.

I remembered the details of the dream. I sat up in bed, running it through my mind, trying to make sense of it.

My watch, on the bedside table, read 4:35. Going back to sleep was out of the question. My mind was roiling. What the hell was my subconscious trying to tell me?

I didn't have a damn clue.

Chapter 24

I lay there on top of the sheets until the numbers on my watch clicked to 5:00. After sitting up and rolling off the bed, I decided to go for a run in the hope that it would clear my head.

I pulled on my sweats and sneakers and made my way quietly down the stairs and out through the kitchen. Winston was already up, dressed in his overalls, and pushing a wheelbarrow loaded with several large bags toward the dairy barn.

"Hey, Al," he said as I stepped off the back porch. "You're up early this morning." He stopped and let the wheelbarrow down.

I jogged over to him. "Yeah, I couldn't sleep, so I thought I'd get in a run before the sun's fully up and it gets too hot."

"Okay, Rowena ought to have her lazy butt up and breakfast goin' by the time you get back."

"Fine," I said. "If she's still cooking, maybe I can give you a hand with your chores when I get back."

He snorted, his wide nose flaring. "Yeah, you do that." Chuckling, he grabbed the wheelbarrow's handles, hefted it up and resumed his journey toward the dairy barn.

Okay, I had that coming I suppose. I've never worked on a farm. We'd been town folks when I was growing up, and unlike most of the kids in my school, I'd never supplemented my income by working on the local farms during harvest time. I delivered newspapers and mowed the occasional lawn, but my mother had been insistent that I would never, and I mean never, work as a field hand. I knew that Winston knew that. In his mind, I'd probably be more hindrance than help, he was just too polite to come right out and say it. Each to his own, I thought. I could do things he couldn't; had, in fact, done things he could never imagine. Thinking that made me feel a little better as I started toward the road at a steady pace.

When I reached the road, I turned right in the direction of the Jarvis farm. By the time I reached the fence boundary between Winston's place and theirs, I was running at a good clip. I did a turn and headed back, pounding hard against the dirt road and kicking up a little cloud of red dust.

By the time I arrived at the back porch, I was breathing hard and sweaty. I ran in place for a few minutes to allow my heartbeat to return to normal and my breathing to slow down. The run had felt good, but it hadn't done a thing for my mental state. I was still thinking about the dream, and I still hadn't a clue what it meant.

I sat cross-legged on the hard-packed earth and meditated for five minutes, and even that didn't help.

Rowena was busy at the stove when I entered the kitchen. She wrinkled her nose and made a face as I walked past her.

"Yeah, I know. I'm pretty ripe after a run, but it makes me feel better."

She pinched her nostrils shut. "Well, you should go take a shower. That'd make you *smell* better. Hurry up, though, breakfast will be ready in a few minutes, and daddy doesn't like having to wait to eat."

"If you get done before I finish showering, just start without me."

"Everyone in the family eats at the same time," she said. "So quit your lollygagging and go wash up."

I never knew Winston's wife, Rowena's mother, but I think Rowena got her personality from her. Winston wasn't the 'giving orders' type, preferring to use his facial expressions to convey his mood. Rowena, on the other hand, verbalized her every thought.

While I was tempted to ask her how someone who lived on a farm that raised cows and chickens with the rank odor that wafted from their enclosures could be sensitive to the odor of exercise-generated sweat, but the 'don't mess with me' look on her face dissuaded me. I went up and took a long, hot shower, and changed into jeans and a brown polo shirt. I even put on a clean pair of socks.

She said nothing, just smiled, when I came back down for breakfast. I noticed that Winston, except for clean hands, looked like someone who'd just come from mucking out a stable. I guess when you're head of the household a different set of rules apply. I, of course, said nothing about this. After all, even though I was family, I was also a guest, and it would have been churlish of me to complain.

The food, consisting of pancakes, sausage patties, scrambled eggs, and coffee, was done to perfection. We ate in silence. After we'd finished, I offered to help Rowena with the dishes. She thankfully declined my offer. Winston, on the other hand, hadn't forgotten my offer to help him with chores.

"I got to change the straw in the dairy barn, and the Martinez boys are busy feeding the chickens," he said. "You want to help me with that?"

That sounded like work, but not too mentally demanding.

"Sure. When do we start?"

He finished his coffee with a slurping sound and put his cup down. "Right now's as good a time as any."

He rose and headed for the back door. I followed.

We were halfway to the dairy barn when I heard the crunch of tires on the hard earth in front of the house, and the growl of a high-performance engine.

"I wonder who that is," Winston said. He turned toward the sound.

"Sounds like you have a visitor."

As I followed him around the house, I wondered if maybe it was Caldwell come to press his case for Winston to sell his land.

When we came around the corner, though, I was taken aback. It wasn't Caldwell's BMW. It was a brown and cream Crown Victoria with a red and blue light bar on top and a gold shield on the door with a single white star and the words 'Coquilla County Sheriff's Department' arced around the star and 'Sheriff' across the base of the shield. It came to a stop in a cloud of red dust, and the engine made ticking sounds for a few seconds after the ignition was turned off.

The driver side door opened and a pair of scuffed brown cowboy boots swung out and kicked up more dust. The owner of the boots stood upright and faced us. He was about five-ten and thin, looking like he weighed in at about one-forty, considerably less if you removed the badge, the bent-brim gray Stetson, and the .44 caliber six-shooter he wore slung low on his hips. His brown uniform hung on him like clothing on a wire hanger. He took off his hat, and the morning sun reflected off his shiny bald onion-shaped head. He looked at us with his thin lips in a half smile and a hard look in his dark brown eyes. He had a hawk nose and sunken cheeks, and the darkness of five o'clock shadow. He was one of those people whose age is impossible to guess. He could've been anywhere from forty to sixty.

"Mornin' Winston," he said in a nasal voice. "Fine mornin' we're havin', ain't it?"

"That it is, Sheriff Danton," Winston said. "Been good weather for quite a spell."

"Keep up like this and you'll have good crops this season."

"That's what I'm hopin' for." Winston cleared his throat. "What brings you out this way, sheriff?"

"Well, Winston, it's like this. I got me a little problem." He looked at me as he spoke.

There was something going on between them, I would have said some tension, but I didn't sense tension.

"Anything I can do to help you with it?" To his credit, Winston didn't look at me.

"I hear you got a cousin from up north visitin', Winston. Would this be him by any chance?"

"That's right. This here's my cousin, Al Pennyback."

Now, Danton was staring directly at me. His bony hand rested on the butt of the revolver. "Pennyback? Don't recollect a family from these parts by that name."

"He ain't from here. His folks lived up in Shelby County."

Danton nodded and rubbed his left hand across the stubble on his pointed chin.

"Well, that explains why the name didn't ring a bell."

"You said you had a problem?"

"Oh, yeah, I do." Now his attention was only on me. "You know a fella named Loren Caldwell, Mr. Pennyback?"

"Yes, he's the gentleman who *claims* to work for an outfit called GeoSync, and he's trying to buy a chunk of land from my cousin here."

"Yep, that's him all right," Danton said. "Now, here's the problem I got. Mr. Caldwell says that you pressured people who'd agreed to sell to him, causin' 'em to back out of the deal."

Winston stepped forward. "That's a—" I put a hand on his chest and shook my head.

"Mr. Caldwell misinformed you sheriff," I said.

"You didn't talk people out of sellin' him their land?"

I had to answer this one carefully. I wasn't sure how this involved the sheriff, but I didn't want to get crosswise with the local law here in Podunkville.

"It's not as simple as that, sheriff. I advised my cousin to hold off on making a decision, of course, and I also talked to one of the other sellers, Angus Murphy. I told Mr. Murphy I thought there was something fishy about the offer and that he might want to hold off on selling until we know more. I've never met any of the other potential sellers."

"Now, let me see if I got this straight. You only talked to Angus Murphy, and you convinced him to hold off on sellin'?"

"Correct."

"You sure you didn't use a little . . . pressure on him?"

I didn't like his tone of voice, and I definitely didn't like where I sensed this was going. "I'm positive I didn't use any pressure," I said, fighting to keep my voice even. "In fact, we had quite a pleasant conversation." Then, I took a leap of faith. "Did he tell you different?"

He blinked. Ah ha! He hadn't even talked to Murphy.

"Did you even *talk* to Mr. Murphy?" I asked.

The widening of his eyes was almost imperceptible—almost—but, I saw it, and he *knew* that I'd seen it.

"Well . . . naw, I hadn't got 'round to speakin' to him just yet," he said. He broke eye contact with me and looked down at his boots.

"Don't you think that before you come and accuse me of what amounts to assault on someone you should interview the alleged victim?"

His cheeks darkened, and he whipped his head up and locked gazes with me. "I didn't accuse you of anything. I was just askin' a question, is all."

"Sho 'nuff sounded like you was accusin' to me," Winston said.

Danton shifted his gaze from me to Winston. The two of them glared at each other like two old bulls facing off in a pasture full of cows. I held a hand up.

"Hold up. I might have misspoke. It *sounded* like you were accusing me of using coercion. I can assure you I didn't, but you can get that information directly from Angus Murphy and it should put your mind at rest."

"Reckon I could drop in on him."

"You could call him," Winston said. "I got me one of them new speaker phones you can use. You know his number?"

"I reckon Directory Assistance can get if for me. Okay, I'll call from here."

Winston led us into the living room. He pointed the phone out to Danton. "You know how to use one of these?" he asked.

Danton gave him a withering glare. "I might be a bit old, but I ain't completely behind the times, Winston Jones. If an old coot like you know how to use one, I'm pretty sure I can figure it out."

"Well, in that case, come on in and take it for a spin."

Winston turned and walked up the steps to the front porch. The sheriff followed, and I followed him. Rowena came in from the kitchen just as we entered the living room.

"Hey, Rowena," Danton said. "You home for summer vacation?"

"Yeah, I am, Sheriff Danton," she said, smiling broadly. "How you been doing?"

"Aw, not too bad, 'cept my arthritis been actin' up lately, and that boy of mine's still drivin' me crazy."

"I hear he got admitted to Rice."

"Yeah, and he just barely made a B average this year. You think you could speak to him for me this summer? He's supposed to be comin' home this weekend."

"Sure, be happy to. You want something cold to drink?"

"Well, I sure could use a glass of your iced tea . . . if it ain't no bother."

"No bother at all. How about you and Al, daddy, y'all want tea too?"

"Sho nuff, baby girl," Winston said.

I nodded, not really paying much attention to what she said, confused by the familiar way Rowena and the sheriff interacted.

"Now, Winston," the sheriff said; now smiling. "Where's this new-fangled phone of yours."

"Over there on the sideboard." Winston pointed to the beige phone. "Help yourself."

Danton crossed the room and picked up the receiver. He pressed a few buttons and put the receiver to his ear. "Hi, darlin'," he said after a few seconds. "Can you give me the number for Angus Murphy here in Poseyville? You can do that? Why that's plumb nice of you." He put his hand over the mouthpiece. "She's gon' put me through to the number instead of makin' me dial it myself." He paused. "It's ringin'. I'll put it on speaker so y'all can hear both sides of the conversation . . . uh, hello, hang on a minute." He pushed the 'loudspeaker' on the face of the instrument.

"Hello, who is this?" The voice sounded a bit tinny from the phone's tiny speaker, but I recognized Angus Murphy.

"This is Coquilla County Sheriff Beauregard Danton, who'm I speakin' to?"

"Hey, sheriff, this is Angus Murphy, why you callin' me?"

"Hey, Angus, I'm callin' to ask you if you know a gentleman by the name of Al Pennyback."

"Sure do. He come by my place t'other day. Why?"

"Why'd he come to visit you?"

"He said this fella name of Caldwell offerin' to buy some land off his cousin. My neighbor, Nancy Jo Billings done told him the same fella was tryin' to buy a piece of my land, and she sent him to talk to me 'bout it."

Danton looked at me, and I swear he had a smile on his face.

"Did this Pennyback fella try to pressure you *not* to sell your land?"

"Pressure? Naw, he ain't done nothin' like that. He did tell me, though, that he thought maybe Caldwell was up to somethin', and maybe I oughter take a closer look at it 'fore I sign the land away. Way he said it, made a lot of sense, so I done just that."

"He didn't threaten you or anything?"

"Naw. In fact, he was quite well-mannered. He even took the time to sit down and have a drink with an old man. Ain't too many young uns do that nowadays, you know."

Danton nodded and made 'hm' noises. "I do know. Look, Angus, do you know if he talked to any of the other folks that were plannin' to sell land to Caldwell?"

"I don't think so," Murphy said. "But, I sure's hell did, and they felt the same way I did. We's all holdin' off on finalizin' the sales until Caldwell answers some tough questions. Why you askin' all these questions, sheriff?"

"Well, Angus, I was led to believe that Pennyback strong armed you and the others not to sell your land."

"I don't know who you got that from, sheriff, but that's a pure-dee lie. You know me, and you know I ain't one you can easy pressure."

"Yeah, I did find it passin' strange. Well, thanks for your time, Angus. You take care, hear?"

He put the receiver and turned to me.

"Well, Mr. Pennyback, it appears I still got me a problem, only it ain't with you."

"Uh huh," Winston said. "It 'pears to me, it's this Caldwell fella who got the problem. Ain't such a good idea lyin' to the law."

"Naw, it ain't," Danton said. "Mr. Pennyback, you up to takin' a little trip?"

"Where to?"

"I thought we'd drive into town and have a little chat with Loren Caldwell."

He had a wolfish grin on his face.

"I'll get my keys and be right behind you, sheriff."

Danton was waiting at the bottom of the porch steps for me when I returned with the keys.

"Before we get there, we need to discuss something," he said.

"What's that, sheriff?"

"We gonna do a little play-acting. Until that bastard cracks, I don't want you to do or say anything to make him think I don't suspect he might not've been tellin' the truth about you."

That brought me up short. "Whoa," I said. "Are you saying that you suspected all along he was lying?"

"Not when he first told me, but when he said you was Winston's kin, I knew he was spinning me a yarn."

"Oh, why's that?"

"Look, son, I've known Winston most of my life. That old reprobate might be a lot of things, but one thing he ain't is a liar, and he don't abide any of his kin lying either. Sorry if I come on a little hard, but I just wanted to make sure. And, I was pretty sure soon's you opened your mouth that you was as truthful as your cousin."

"Sounds like you and Winston . . . get along."

"Hell, sure we do. Me'n Winston been best friends since we was tadpoles."

"But, the way you talk to each other—"

"Aw, you mean 'cause we ain't all gushy and shit," he said. "Hell, that just ain't our way. We been snipin' at each like that long's I can remember. Ain't neither one of us much for the soapy stuff, but I'd risk my life for that man, and I'm pretty sure he'd do the same for me."

I'd had buddies in the army like that. Men who were closer than brothers who could never say 'I love you,' but who loved with every fiber of their being; the kind of brotherly love that doesn't need words. I felt like kicking myself. Some detective I was, not noticing that beneath their gruffness as they spat insults at each other, there was a kind of tenderness.

"Shit, I'm sorry, sheriff," I said.

"For what?"

"For what I was thinking about you a while ago."

He laughed. "Shit, son, don't think nothin' of it. I reckon folks what don't know us might get the wrong idea. Don't matter. Our friendship ain't nobody else's business. We probably do that 'cause back when we was kids, a white boy and a colored boy bein' such close friends wasn't exactly looked at too kindly."

I could imagine it wouldn't have. I remember my own childhood in East Texas. Folks were kindly enough, but when whites and blacks came into contact, there was always a kind of unspoken agreement, they would do what had to be done and move back to their separate worlds. There *were* those whites who would only deal with other races in a situation of superior to subordinate, and a few who wouldn't under any circumstances. The ones that my grandmother called 'the good white folks' were kind enough, even going so far as to attend black funerals, but always sat separated from the rest of us, and left immediately after tendering their condolences. They were never harsh or imperious with us, and always seemed nervous when around us, but kept the contact to a minimum. What must it have been like for Beauregard Danton and Winston Jones, two boys from completely different, and somewhat antagonistic, worlds to be friends with each other? I couldn't even imagine it, other than it must have been like being in a war.

"How did you two become friends?" I asked.

"When I was a boy, my daddy had the farm on the other side of Winston's place—daddy sold it the year I graduated from high school, 'cause he got too sick to work it, and I was goin' off to the army—and I was messin' 'round down near the edge of the swamp right at the fence line between our place and Winston's daddy's farm. Anyway's, I got stuck in quicksand. I was about six or seven at the time, and Winston must've been maybe ten, but even then he was big and strong. He heard me screamin' for help, and come over the fence and pulled me out of that quicksand. Saved my life, he did. We been friends ever since."

"Wow, all those times when he was a teenager and used to come visit us, he never mentioned he had a white friend."

"Well, I reckon it was somethin' neither of us ever talked about to others. I ain't sure my daddy would've cared one way or t'other, but some of his friends would've been scandalized. Same for Winston, I reckon.

Anyway, we used to go off huntin' or fishin' 'long the creek on weekends 'till I graduated and joined the army. I went off and spent four years in the army, I got out just 'fore that mess in Vietnam started, and come back home. Daddy had died while I was in the army, and the farm got sold off, so I got me a job as a deputy sheriff with the county. Winston's mama and daddy had done died, and he was workin' his farm, so we picked up where we left off, until the old sheriff got sick about fifteen years ago and had me put my name in the hat to run in his place. Folks elected me, and been re-electin' me ever since, so I been too busy to see Winston more'n ever couple months. We still get together and go fishin' whenever I can get time off. We fish in the stream where it comes out of the swamp."

"Damn, you two sure had me fooled." I shook my head. "You're pretty good, sheriff, I'll give you that."

"Hey, Al, call me Bo except when we're talkin' to Caldwell," he said. "I want him to think I still believe the shit he told me. That way, it'll be more fun when we trip him up."

"Sheriff, Bo, you do have a devious mind. I like it. Let's roll."

I had a feeling this *was* going to be fun.

Charles Ray

Chapter 25

Nancy Jo Billings looked up in surprise when Danton and I entered the office.

"Well, morning, sheriff," she said. "What're you doing here in Poseyville this morning?" Then, she saw me, and a momentary frown flickered, but was quickly replaced by a smile. "Good morning, Mr. Pennyback."

"Mornin', Nancy Jo," Danton said. He looked at me with a half-smile on his face. The man was quick on the uptake, I had to give him that. "You know I like to get around the county as much as possible. How's your momma these days?"

"She's fine." She spoke to him, but looked at me.

"I see you know Mr. Pennyback here."

"Uh, yes, he's visited us here," she said. Her cheeks went red. "I believe Mr. Caldwell's buying some land from his cousin."

"Speaking of Mr. Caldwell, is he in?"

"Yes." She reached for the phone. "I'll let him know—"

Danton put a hand on hers, stopping her from lifting the phone. "Naw, it won't be necessary to announce us," he said. "We'll just go on in. Now, you take care, you hear, and say hello to your momma for me."

She pulled her hand away from the phone and looked wide-eyed at me. I winked, which caused her brow to wrinkle. 'Don't worry,' I mouthed, and followed Danton as he pushed through the door to Caldwell's office.

Caldwell was sitting behind his desk, reading from a sheet of bond paper he held in front of his face as if he had problem focusing on it. He looked over the top of the paper, and when he saw the sheriff, he smiled, and then I came into view, and his smile took a nosedive, turning into a genuine frown.

"Morning, sheriff," he said. "What's he doing here?" The *he* he referred to was me, and he made that clear by putting the paper down and jabbing an index finger in my direction.

"Well now, Loren, you don't mind if I call you Loren do you? Anyway, Loren, you made a pretty serious accusation against Al here." He turned so Caldwell couldn't see his face and waggled his eyebrows at me. I got the message. I kept my mouth shut, prepared to follow his lead. "Now, in these here United States, the accused has got the right to confront his accuser. Here in Coquilla County, we pride ourselves on followin' the law to the letter. So, I brought Al here to confront you about your accusations."

Caldwell's expression changed from irritation to confusion. I could almost sympathize with him. I had absolutely no idea where Danton was going with this.

"Uh, I don't understand," Caldwell said.

"It's like this, Loren. I'm gon' ask a few questions, and you and Al each git to answer them. That way, I 'spect we'll right quickly git to the bottom of this situation. That sound fair to you, Al?"

"Sounds perfectly fair to me, sheriff," I said with a deadpan expression on my face.

"What about you, Loren? You okay with that?" Danton faced Caldwell with his hands on his hips and an 'aw shucks' smile on his face.

Beads of sweat glistened on Caldwell's forehead. He ran a hand through his hair, looking down at his desk. Finally, he looked up at the sheriff. "Uh, yeah, I guess that's okay," he said.

"Why don't we all sit down and get comfortable," Danton said. He walked around and turned the chair to the left of Caldwell's desk around, and straddled it, resting his arms across the back. I took the chair to the right. Caldwell looked from one of us to the other like a spectator at a tennis match, the expression on his face that of a man who has placed a bet on the match's outcome; on the player who is losing. "Okay," Danton said. "Here's the first question, and it's for you, Al. Did you pay a visit to Angus Murphy?"

"Yes I did," I said. "I went to his house yesterday."

Danton nodded his head, his Adam's apple bobbing up and down in time with the movements of his bald pate.

"Good, very good. See how that works, Loren?" Caldwell nodded. "Now, my next question's also for Al. Al, why did you visit Angus?"

I repeated what I'd already told him, leaving out the part about Nancy Jo being the one who'd pointed me toward him.

"Did you threaten him in any way?" Danton asked.

"No, I did not."

He pointed a finger at Caldwell. "Now, Loren, you see the problem I have here, don't you? You told me that Al here coerced Angus into cancelling the sale of his property to you."

"Yeah, I did, and he did. He's lying," Caldwell said.

"Now, that's one of them 'your word against his' kind of situations. You say he did, he says he didn't. Who am I gonna believe?"

"Oh, come on sheriff. Are you gonna take *his* word over mine?"

The way he smirked and glared at me as he spoke I got his meaning as clear as if he'd put up a neon sign. He was playing the 'good old boy' card. For a moment, the way Danton was bobbing his head I thought it might be working, but I'd underestimated just how devious the old man could be.

"I gotta admit, you make a point, Loren. Even though you're from Lufkin, and not exactly local, you are a Texas boy sort of, while Al here might've been born in Texas, but he left and, now, he's from up north."

"That's right, and he's come down here sticking his nose where it doesn't belong. He interfered with my business."

"I reckon that's part right," Danton said. "You did interfere with his business, Al. Wouldn't you admit that's correct?"

I nodded again. "I guess I have to confess that what I did could be considered interfering."

"You see, sheriff, I told you. He's as much as admitted it."

Danton wagged that finger again.

"That he did, Loren. But, you see, *interferin'* with your business ain't exactly the same as threatin' somebody. Interferin' ain't hardly illegal, 'cause if it was, half the big companies in the state would be in court. I believe that's just called free enterprise, or competition, or just tough titty."

"B-but, he just admitted that he coerced old man Murphy to cancel the sale."

"Now, that ain't the way I heard it. I heard him say he suggested to Angus that he might want to hold off on sellin' to you."

"Of course he wouldn't *admit* that he threatened the old man, but I think there's enough circumstantial evidence to assume that's what he did."

"Are you a lawyer, Loren? You ever work in law enforcement?"

"Uh, no."

"Didn't think so. There ain't no evidence indicatin' to me that Al threatened anyone, much less Angus Murphy. In fact, the evidence seems to point in the opposite direction."

"What evidence is that?"

Danton chuckled. "Direct testimony from Angus Murphy himself," he said. "I talked to him, and got the same story you just heard from Al."

"Maybe the old man's just confused . . . or scared. Besides, Pennyback here also got to the other buyers and scared them off too."

"No, Angus said he's the one did that."

"I don't even know the names of any of the other buyers," I offered.

Danton stood, again with his hands on his hips. "And, that brings me to another problem, Loren, a real big problem. I might just be a small-time sheriff in a poor rural county, but I get kind of peeved when somebody tries to play me. Lying to law enforcement and filin' a false report; now, *that* is a crime."

Caldwell looked deflated. He sank back in his chair. "B-but, sheriff, I didn't try to . . . play you. Okay, okay, maybe I made a mistake, and Pennyback didn't actually coerce those farmers, but you can see my situation. I've been working hard to close these sales, and right after he starts nosing around it all falls apart."

"You know, I *could* charge you with filing a false report."

Caldwell shrank even further into his chair and his face paled.

"I bet your bosses at Global Energy would really like that," I said.

They both whirled to face me; Danton looking confused, and Caldwell with a look of panic.

"Sheriff, please, I apologize for any inconvenience. I would hope you could see your way clear to forgive me," Caldwell said. "I didn't intentionally file a false report."

"Did you say Global Energy?" Danton asked me, and ignoring him.

Chapter 26

"That's right, sheriff," I said. "Mr. Caldwell here claims to work for an outfit called GeoSync, but my partner back in DC has been unable to find any such organization in any database in the world, and trust me, if she can't find it, that's because it doesn't exist. What she did discover is that Loren Caldwell is listed as an executive of Global Energy in Lufkin."

"Is that a fact? Loren, do you work for Global Energy?"

"Uh, well, I did once, but I quit to go to work for GeoSync."

"To work for an organization that doesn't exist?" I asked.

"Just because you can't find it doesn't prove it doesn't exist."

"Unfortunately, he has a point there, Al," Danton said.

Caldwell's fear was replaced by a look of smugness at that point. But, I knew something he didn't know I knew, something that I hoped would wipe the smug look right off his face.

"When did you leave Global?" I asked.

"I told you, six months ago," he said.

I looked at Danton and smiled. "You know, you and your buddy should've done a better job of rehearsing your legends," I said.

"What the hell does that mean?" he asked.

"According to your buddy, Alan Grayson, chief of security for Global, and your old army buddy, you quit over a year ago," I said.

The smug look fled his face like a rabbit that just saw a fox come around a turn in the trail. It was replaced by a stricken look, a look that Danton didn't miss.

"Is that a fact?" Danton said. "Which is it, Loren, six months or over a year? Can't be both, now can it?"

"I, uh, I mean my employment officially ended six months ago, because of the terms of my contract. I actually left the company just a little over a year ago to work for GeoSync." His ability to spin glib lies seemed to have deserted him. Sometimes when you're fast on your feet, you trip all over them, which is what he was doing.

"I ain't never heard of that kind of deal," Danton said. "Now, Al, you say this partner of yours says there's no such organization as GeoSync?"

"That's right, sheriff. My partner, Heather, is a computer expert. If she does a computer search on you, she finds out things about you that sometimes even you don't know. If she says the organization doesn't exist, it doesn't exist. Think about it, an organization studying ancient geology or whatever, that can afford to pay ten thousand bucks an acre for essentially worthless land, can't be hidden. If nothing else, it has to have a bank account. I doubt you carry half a million in cash around with you, do you, Caldwell?"

Danton's mouth dropped open. "Half a million? You're offering half a million for farm land here in Poseyville?"

"For five plots," I said before Caldwell could answer. "And, not really farm land. In the cases of my uncle and Angus Murphy, he's offering to buy totally worthless land, swamp and bog mostly, at ten thousand dollars an acre."

"Okay, Loren, it's your turn to answer questions now," Danton said, and his tone was now stern. The good old boy persona had mostly disappeared, and he was all cop. "Al was pretty forthcoming with his answers, so I hope you're gon' be doin' the same. How come you're paying so much money for land that won't grow nothin'?"

"It's for scientific research, sheriff." Caldwell was sticking to a story that now had so many holes in it I could hear the wind whistling through it.

"Son, stop right there. Now, I already said I don't like it when somebody thinks I'm just some dumb hick sheriff that don't know his ass from his elbow. I might live in a little town, and I don't have a fancy college degree like you probably have, but I know bullshit when I hear it. Less'n you work for the CIA or the Pentagon, there ain't no way in hell you got that kinda money to throw 'round for no scientific research. You gon' have to do better than that."

Caldwell just stood there, his mouth opening and closing like a fish out of water. The color had completely drained from his face.

"Well, come on, boy, spit it out." All traces of the good old boy had faded from Danton's voice now. He was now a hard-bitten cop, grilling a suspect that he knows damned well is guilty. "You still work for Global Energy, don't you? And, don't even think about lyin' to me again, boy, 'cause that would piss me off, and trust me, you don't want to piss me off."

A single tear leaked out of the corner of his left eye and flowed slowly down his cheek, to drip off his chin. He looked deflated, completely shrunken with all the gas sucked out.

"W-what do you plan to do?" he asked in a quiet voice.

"Now, that sorta depends on what you got to say, boy."

"Are you arresting me?"

"I could run you in for filing a false report," Danton said. "But, that's just a misdemeanor, and ain't hardly worth all the paperwork. On the other hand, you're buyin' land under false pretenses, and that could be construed as fraud, and that my boy is a felony. Now, that one might be worth pursuin', 'cause it'd get you some real hard time."

Caldwell ducked his head back as if he'd been slapped.

"No, no, it's not like that. We, I mean, Global is offering above market value for the land. That's not fraud."

"So, you admit you work for Global?"

"Yeah, yeah, I work for Global Energy." He was deflated now. All the bravado was gone.

Danton snorted through his nose like an angry bull. "So, why in damnation you goin' 'round pretendin' to work for some other company? And, why ain't you leasin' the land like the oil companies usually do?"

"Blame the bean counters." Caldwell shrugged. "Some joker in accounting decided it was simpler and in the long run more profitable for the company if we just bought the land outright instead of signing a complicated leasing agreement."

Bingo! The nature of his scam fell neatly into place.

"So, this way, if the oil or gas under the land turns out to be really lucrative, the former land owner wouldn't get quite as much as they would if they were leasing," I said. "But, since you paid them over market value for the land, they wouldn't really have grounds to complain too much."

He gave me an approving nod. I guess he thought I was admiring his slickness.

"That's right," he said. "And, one of the clauses in the purchase agreement transfers *all* mineral rights to the purchaser, in this case me. Of course, I then immediately transfer title to Global."

Danton shook his head. His nostrils were flaring.

"Dammit to hell, it's still cheatin', son," he said. "It might not be enough for me to throw your sorry ass in jail, but it's enough for me to tell you not to let the sun set on your ass in Coquilla County."

"Sheriff, might I propose an alternative," I said.

"One that lets this son of a bitch continue to pollute the air of my county with his presence?"

"Well, just for a short while longer. There's no sense in the people of Poseyville not getting something out of this."

He looked at me through narrow slits. "I'm listening," he said.

My proposal was simple; accompany Caldwell around to each of the landowners, only, instead of offering to buy their land, offer to lease it for mineral development, with a fair share of the profits therefrom going to the landowner. If there was something worthwhile under the soil, Global would still make a pile of money, but so would the landowners. In addition, I suggested that the lease agreement include a clause requiring the company to restore the land to its original state if nothing was found.

"This way," I said when I'd finished describing my proposal. "Everyone benefits."

"The honchos at Global aren't going to like it," Caldwell said. "They've become pretty committed to the simpler method of buying it outright."

"They're not going to have that option any longer," I said. "Once word gets out, there's probably not a person in the state who'd sell you land."

"Besides," Danton said. "It ain't like you have much of a choice. You can stay in Poseyville long enough to present lease proposals and sign any necessary papers, or you can get your ass out of town by sundown. You think your bosses would like *that?*"

He sounded like one of those sheriffs from an old western movie, laying down the law to the desperado, and the way he twiddled his fingers on the butt of his revolver, he looked like one.

Caldwell sighed deeply. "Okay, okay, I'll do it."

"Kinda thought you'd see reason," Danton said. "Now, you go on and git them papers ready, and I'll be back here directly so we can start out. Reckon we ought to be finished by noon tomorrow, don't you?"

Caldwell sat there, nodding dumbly and looking defeated, making me want to smack his face. Sure, I'd collapsed his house of cards, but it wasn't like I'd really hurt him. His company still stood to make a ton of money out of the deal, but this way, the poor schmucks who now owned the land could benefit as well.

"Okay, sheriff," he said. "I should have all the leasing agreements ready for signature by 2:30."

"Then, I'll see you at 2:30." Danton put his hat on, touched a fingertip to the brim and walked out of the office with me in his wake.

In the outer office he stopped in front of a befuddled looking Nancy Jo Billings' desk.

"Nancy Jo," he said. "You're gon' be busy probably for the rest of the day, but I don't think you'll have a job here tomorrow. I'm sorry for that, but if there's anything I can do, you just call me."

She looked from him to me with questions in her eyes.

"Mr. Caldwell will be returning to Lufkin to his job at Global Energy," I said. "I think this office will be closed for good."

She beamed a broad smile as comprehension dawned.

"Well, I was working as the main receptionist over at Piggly Wiggly before Mr. Caldwell came to town. I'm pretty sure Bobby, the general manager, will give me my old job back."

"Bobby Lee Pickins?" Danton said. "Why, he's a second cousin on my daddy's side . . . or is it my momma . . . can't hardly ever remember; anyway, don't matter, I'll have a word with him, Nancy Jo. Consider the job yours."

She was fairly glowing when we left the office.

Family and friends. In small towns they always come first.

Chapter 27

I got back to Winston's place just in time for an early lunch. When I told him what had transpired, he made the decision then and there to accept the lease offer, and I couldn't blame him. It would provide much-needed money for repairs, take care of Rowena's college expenses, and even leave some money set aside for Winston's retirement—provided there *was* oil or gas, or whatever the hell Global was looking for, under the ground. And, Winston would still be keeping the family estate intact. That, I knew, was what was really important to him.

With Caldwell nicely boxed in, that only left the mystery of Dudley Jarvis and his fixation with my cousin's swamp; my final puzzle, and I was determined to solve it.

At 2:30, just about the time Beauregard Danton would be picking Caldwell up at his office, I was in my bedroom, dressing for a daytime trip to the swamp.

First, I pulled on black cargo pants and a long-sleeved black shirt, both of heavy-duty, but breathable cotton, and then I put on a thick pair of black cotton socks. I pulled the hip waders on over this and fastened the shoulder straps snugly. This time, instead of trying to attach my knife to a boot, I clipped it to the left shoulder strap of the waders where I could easily reach it. I was just about to walk out of the room when I decided to take the alligator gig along, must in case I ran into a gator hungry for a snack.

I bumped into Winston on my way out the back door. He frowned at me. "Don't tell me you goin' in that swamp again."

"Okay, I won't tell you."

"Aw, Al, how many times I gotta tell you, it's dangerous down there."

I held up the gig. "I think I can handle snakes and a few gators," I said.

"Yeah? What about the haints?"

"Look, Winston, I saw a light when I was down there the other night, but it was no ghost, it was someone with a lantern or flashlight."

"How do you know that? Did you get close enough to see? Wait, you think it was a person?"

"No, but I didn't have to get close to know I wasn't seeing a ghost—even if I believed in such things. I've been on enough combat patrols to know a hand-held light when I see one, and what I saw was a hand-held light. Someone was prowling around your property at night, and the way that light was moving, they've been there before."

"Shit," he said. "You think it was that Caldwell fella, snoopin' 'round down there?"

"I don't see Caldwell as the type to get dirty. I think it was someone else."

"Who the hell else would be sneakin' 'round my place?"

"Your neighbor, Dudley Jarvis, for one," I said. "I think he's the one prowling the swamp."

"Dudley? Why'n hell would that cracker be messin' 'round down there?"

"I don't know, Winston. That's why I'm going down there now. I need to be able to see clearly, so I'm doing it in daylight."

"You be careful, Al," he said. "If he is doin' somethin' bad, ain't no tellin' what he might do if he see you."

I held the gig up. "Don't worry, I plan on seeing him first. Hey, cuz, this isn't my first rodeo."

With that, I left him standing there with a skeptical look on his face. I was serious, though. I didn't want Jarvis to see me before I saw him, so I angled toward the side of the swamp farthest from his property. My plan was to enter there, and work my way in a criss-cross pattern toward his place. I had no idea what I was looking for, so I'd just have to look for anomalies, which meant I'd be going slow. Add to that the need to keep an eye out for him, and it meant I'd be going *really* slow. I figured it'd be close to nightfall by the time I finished; not dark enough to need a flashlight—hopefully.

I walked along the fence line where the going was faster. I had the added advantage for the first three-quarters of the way of the corn blocking the view from Jarvis's side. The open area before the trees was dicey. I waited in the tall crops, scanning to make sure there was no one in sight, and then made a dash for the trees—not easy to do when you're wearing waders.

Once in the trees, I stopped for a moment and leaned against the trunk of a tree to catch my breath and get my bearings. The big trees provided shade, but the temperature was already approaching three digits, and with the moisture in the air here, the shade was useless. The heat was beginning to suck the energy out of me through every pore in my body. I was wet from top to bottom, and could feel the rivulets of sweat rolling down my back, arms and legs, as well as the moisture on my feet seeping through my socks and pooling in the bottom of the wader's boots. I wiped at the sweat pouring off my brow, and only succeeded in smearing it around and getting the salty liquid in my eyes, along with a bit of grit that stung like the dickens. This was, I could see, going to be a long, arduous trek. But, there was nothing for it but to do it. I pushed off from the tree and began walking in the direction of the stream.

In the cool of the night a swamp's a noisy place, with insects chirping, frogs croaking, and the whistles of birds and the occasional grunt of an alligator. But, when it's hot and muggy, animals are smart. They find a shady place to hole up and sit, squat, perch, or lie quietly, conserving their energy for their later hunts for food. The sound of my breathing was unnaturally loud in the gloomy quiet, and the warm, moisture-laden air I was sucking into my nostrils felt like syrup, only it was salty, not sweet.

For the first hundred yards, as I made my way down toward the stream and back, I waded through lukewarm water that varied from ankle deep to lapping at my butt, having to walk in a zigzag line because of the tangled vegetation. With every step, I kept a wary eye out for any signs of a moccasin cutting through the water at me, or the nose holes, eyes, and bumpy head of an alligator, which is all I would be likely to see until just before one of these prehistoric monsters erupted from the water to catch me in its jaws..

Then, the terrain changed. There were still wide pools of fetid, green-scum covered water, some coming up almost to my waist, but most no more than knee-deep, but there were also many hummocks of land, some no more than a basket-ball sized hump with a small tree growing from it, but others big enough to hold a basketball court, irregularly-shaped plots of grown littered with trees and bramble bushes. Some were low and soggy. Some were elevated high enough to be dry and solid. I saw animal signs, birds' nests, tracks in the soft ground, dry droppings, but nothing worrying.

I was just turning back toward the stream, in an area that was, by swamp standards, mostly dry, when I saw it.

A relatively flat expanse of ground, sparsely covered by stunted trees and clumps of brush, it was high enough that five feet away from the shallow, brackish water surrounding it, the earth was hard-packed and light brown. From there down to the water, it was cracked showing the water level had fallen at some time in the past.

It was the impression in one relatively soft area, though, that caught my eye. Rounded toward the water, with straight sides, it was just clear enough for me to recognize it as a boot print, a mark made by someone headed toward the center of the land mass, where I could see a large clear area of light brown earth, and a large dead tree, about fifty feet tall with its grey limbs spread out and reaching for earth and sky like bony grey fingers. There was no telling when the mark had been made, but it had to be relatively recent, at least since the last rain. Of course, it hadn't rained since my arrival in Poseyville, so as far as I knew, it could have been made only hours earlier. That didn't matter really. It showed that someone had been here, and what I *did* know was that it wasn't me, and the print was too small to have been made by Winston, who was unlikely to have come this deep into the swamp in any case.

This area was well inside Winston's land. Someone had been here. How many times? Impossible to tell. But, that was less important than the mere fact that someone *had* been here.

I decided to explore the interior of this hummock.

As I moved slowly toward the center of the area, a number of possibilities swam through my mind. The first was that maybe someone was using this isolated area for some illegal activity. Even though Coquilla County, like most counties in East Texas, was no longer dry as they'd been when I was a kid, bootlegging was still an active underground activity for many. There was also a healthy traffic in illegal drugs and other contraband coming up from Mexico, through East Texas, headed for points north. And finally, I'd heard of illegal drug manufacturing operations, principally methamphetamine labs, in this part of the country. Any of these meant the possibility of a hostile welcome if I should happen to stumble into the perpetrators, so I moved slowly, scanning each inch of ground to the front and sides with care as I moved forward toward the big dead tree.

I was so busy looking for a building, a still, or some other above-ground structure, I almost missed it. In fact, if it hadn't been for the oddness of it, I might've missed it anyway.

When the earth's been disturbed, the affected soil tends to be slightly darker than the surrounding undisturbed earth, and the ground will be slightly higher or lower than the surrounding earth depending upon how long it's been since it was disturbed. The small, rectangular area of disturbed earth was in front of me. Only a bit darker than the surrounding dirt, it was the evenness of its outline, the long sides aimed at the big tree, which caught my eye just before I would have stepped on it. I took a step backward and looked more closely. The little rectangle was about a quarter of an inch lower than the surrounding ground, meaning it had been dug out a long time ago.

There was no doubt in my mind, though. Someone had dug a hole here. About three feet wide by five feet long, an almost perfect rectangle. The thought of pirate treasure or stolen goods popped into my mind. That would explain Jarvis's concern about the area. Maybe he's a bank robber and this is where he stashes his loot until the heat is off, I thought.

That made perfect sense until I looked to the right and left and noticed similar disturbances to either side of the first, more signs of disturbed earth.

I decided to check the area out more thoroughly, and as I walked around to the right, I began to feel a chill at the back of my neck.

There were more signs of digging, more rectangular disturbed areas, but it was the arrangement that chilled me. They were side by side, about four to six feet apart, and they appeared to be curving around, were in fact curving around, in a large circle, with the big tree at the center. Counting them as I walked, I was at fifty-six when I returned to my footprints in the semi-soft ground. Fifty-six three-by-five rectangles in a large, rough circle around the old dead tree. The thoughts crowding into my mind now were a hell of a lot worse than pirate treasure or stolen loot, and they made an illegal still or drug operation seem pedestrian.

I don't know how I knew, but I *knew.* These were graves. Curious, I walked toward the tree. At its base was a rectangular mound of earth, the same size as those making up the circle around the tree. This one was different in that it was raised above the surrounding ground, and looked definitely like a grave. The way the earth was packed, it looked like it had been tended at some point in the past, and the color of the mound was different from the surrounding dirt. It had been brought there from somewhere else.

The tree served as a kind of tombstone. Withered gray stems lay scattered on the mound at the end nearest the tree.

Damn! This is some kind of burial ground. It can't be Indian. This is not how they honored their dead, and there would be some kind of totems or artifacts. Who the hell is buried here, and even more important, why are they buried here?

The thought repulsed me, but I knew there was only one way to find out. Grasping the handle of the alligator gig and plunging the tines into the earth, I began to dig.

Charles Ray

Chapter 28

I dug gently, scooping the earth out from one of the long sides, until about two feet down, the metal tines of the gig hit something hard. I knelt and grasped the gig just above the tines and began to scrape softly until the bleached white object was uncovered. Using my hands, I brushed dirt away, exposing more of the object. When I realized what it was, I jerked my hand back and gasped. I could feel my lunch gurgling in my stomach. I clenched my jaw to keep from spewing it up and contaminating the scene.

It was a human pelvic bone, small and pitted with smears of green, gray and brown in places. Whoever it was, he or she had lain here for a long time.

Taking a deep breath, I began removing the rest of the earth from the shallow grave, alternating between standing to remove the topsoil, and kneeling to brush dirt away to expose more bones. It took me about twenty minutes, but I'd finally excavated the entire grave. The body, a complete skeleton, with a rusty brass belt buckle in the middle, but not other sign of clothing or shoes, lay supine with the arm bones across the rib cage. The deceased had been small, about five-two, with a small, narrow skull. There was no way of telling if it was male or female, but the absence of any clothing or biological matter other than the bones indicated that it had lain here under the old tree for a long time.

As I stood and started to walk back to the first anomaly, I noticed four depressions nearby, also rectangular, and arrayed in a fan shape around the grave. They were even lower compared to the surrounding ground than the first ones had been. I hadn't seen them when I first approached the grave. The rough grass that grew over them caused them not to be noticeable unless you were standing at the grave looking away from the tree because of the way the ground sloped downwards.

That made a total of at least sixty possible graves, plus the one under the tree. A lot of burials way out here in a swamp, and on my cousin's land. I couldn't help but wonder what Dudley Jarvis's interest or involvement was in all this, and more importantly, who they were.

This would have to be reported to the authorities, of course. Before I did, I decided to explore a few more of the anomalies so that I could confirm what I was beginning to suspect.

I went back to the outer circle, to the first one I'd noticed, and began the slow process of excavation—exhumation—for the next ninety minutes. By the end of that time, I'd revealed ten more skeletons, some with tattered articles of clothing clinging to the bones, or tattered strips of leather and metal grommets, the remains of shoes, and inside the waders, I was now completely soaked through. The dust on my face and hands was now a slimy slurry of reddish mud, and I itched all over. The heat had done its job well and sucked the energy completely out of me. I was breathing hard, and my arms felt like lead. My back and legs ached. The fatigue, though, was as much mental as physical, or the physical fatigue was exacerbated by what I was seeing.

All of the skeletons I uncovered were about the same size and stature. I'd at first thought they were perhaps small adults, but the more I saw, the more I realized that I was looking at young adults or teens, more likely the latter. The relative cleanliness of the bones indicated they'd been in the ground a long, long time, but this didn't strike me as a regular graveyard. Who the hell puts a graveyard in a swamp, and why were none of them in coffins, even rough pine boxes? That fact and the arrangement of the graves told another story, a macabre story that my mind fought against. This smacked of some kind of ritualistic cult.

Death cults are not common, but neither are they as rare as you might think. There was the Jonestown Massacre in Guyana in 1978, when an American, Jim Jones, leader of the People's Temple, ordered some 900 of his American followers to commit suicide. Closer to home, in 1996, a Kentucky teenager, Rod Ferrell, a self-professed vampire, along with his girlfriend and two other teens, bludgeoned his girlfriend's parents to death. What I was seeing here was only rivaled by the Jonestown Massacre. I had to fight to keep from puking my guts out. I'd seen death before, violent, gruesome death, often immediately after it happened, but this scene, those bleached bones all laid out in some unknown cabalistic pattern hit me in the gut like nothing I'd ever experienced before. Death in combat is one thing, but this was pure evil.

I was standing there, looking down at the contents of the tenth grave I'd just uncovered. To say that I was distracted is an understatement. My world had contracted to that clearing. As a result of that distraction I'd violated the first rule of combat; always maintain 360 degree situational awareness. You need to be aware of every sought, sound, and smell if you want to survive; and that sphere of awareness better extend out as far as the range of any weapons that might be used against you.

I'd let my sphere shrink to just that dry hummock. As a result, danger was well within lethal range when my senses detected it.

The first thing, just at the edge of my notice, was when the bird calls that had become just background noise, ceased. I think my brain registered it, but it didn't trigger an alarm. A nanosecond after that, I heard the scuff of a booted foot on hard earth. *That* sound did trigger an alarm. I turned slowly.

Standing there, just fifty feet away, stood Dudley Jarvis. The twin barrels of his shotgun were aimed at my midsection.

"I told you to stay out of this swamp, but you wouldn't listen," he said. His voice was cold, devoid of any feeling. "Now, I'm gon' have to kill you."

Charles Ray

Chapter 29

He was too far away for me to do anything but stare impending death in the face. It's amazing how, even at that distance, the openings in those two barrels looked as big as the end of a howitzer.

"You'll never get away with it, Jarvis," I said. "My cousin knows I'm down here. He'll come looking for me when I don't show up back at the house."

"Ha! He might be worried 'bout you, but I doubt he'll come down here lookin' for you. Old Winston's scairt of ghosts, he is."

"He'll tell the authorities, and they'll come looking." I edged forward, ever so slowly, trying to close the distance.

"Let 'em. You know how many pools of quicksand's in this place? 'Least a dozen that I know of. I drop you in one, and they never find your body."

I waved my hand around. "But, they're likely to find all this."

He blinked and shook his head. That thought hadn't occurred to him. I moved forward another half inch.

He raised the shotgun. "Stop movin'. I see what you tryin' to do. Now, you set down there and let me think this out."

I was buying time, but it still hadn't done me much good. I hadn't closed the gap between us enough to stand a chance of making a move. I wasn't close enough to tell the choke of his shotgun didn't have a choke, so there was no way of knowing the dispersion pattern of the shot. Unless I could get within 10 feet or less, even an inaccurate shot could see hundreds of pellets striking my body—if not more. I was guessing that Jarvis, like most people in the region who used shotguns for bird hunting, used 12 gauge shells, and a one ounce shell has over 2,300 pellets, each .05 inches in diameter. The center of that grouping of pellets at between 10 to 15 feet can nearly blow a man apart. Even half a grouping can blow a limb off. Only by getting in close enough to deflect the barrel and still be outside the cone of dispersion did I have any chance of surviving. I had to get in close or die.

"Look, we can work this out, Jarvis," I said. "Killing me is not gonna solve whatever problem you have."

That sounded weak even to me. The thought was beginning to form in my head that I was facing down a man who'd killed at least a hundred people, and from the size of the skeletons, probably kids. The look of uncertainty in his expression gave me a glimmer of hope—or maybe it was just that facing death, I was grasping at straws.

"I . . . don't know," he said. "I can't let you tell. I don't want to kill you, but I ain't got no other choice."

"There's always a choice, Dudley." I could smell the rank odor of fear in my sweat, and hear the desperation in my voice. I slid forward another half inch. This time, he didn't seem to notice.

"You don't understand. Got no choice. Family always comes first." He seemed to be talking as much to himself as to me. "He ain't hardly worth it, but he *is* family, and I have to look out for him."

Maybe, I could distract him some more, just long enough. "Who are these people buried here, Dudley?"

"They was just boys, the lot of 'em," he murmured. "Just innocent boys, even if they was colored. He hadn't oughter done it, but he was sick in the head."

"Who is he, Dudley?"

"My daddy is who," he said. "He done kilt 'em, ever one of 'em, and he brought 'em down here to be with Joshua."

I don't have a lot of experience with serial killers. Scratch that; I don't have *any* experience with serial killers. I know they're supposed to have brains that are wired differently from the rest of us. But, there was a sadness in his voice that wasn't what I would have expected from someone who could kill . . . a hundred kids.

"How many?" I asked.

"I don't know," he said. "I ain't never counted."

"Didn't your old man ever tell you?"

"Naw, he never did. I don't think he even remembers himself."

What serial killer doesn't keep track of his kills?

"How did they die?"

He looked at me then, his eyes glistening with tears.

"I think he strangled 'em," he said. "Squeezed the life out of 'em with his bare hands."

The nanosecond it took what he said to register was like an eternity. "Why? Why would your father do this, Dudley?"

"I asked him one time, right after I found out he was doin' it. He said it was 'cause grandpa done beat Joshua to death. Most time I asked him 'bout it, he'd start ramblin', and he ain't hardly been able to say nothin' but 'Joshua' since the stroke," he said. Tears flowed freely from his eyes. They find out they put him in jail. I can't let that happen. You understand, don't you? Got to take care of family."

He had that unfocused look in his eyes I'd seen before. Guys who'd been through so many firefights they'd reached the end of their tether to sanity, and who were in another plane of existence. If his father was the one who'd killed all the people—the young boys—in this circle of graves, he was a true monster, certifiably insane, but at this moment, whether he'd ever killed anyone or not, Dudley Jarvis was also a complete fruitcake; and one of the most dangerous kinds, one with a deadly weapon. And, here I was, still too far away to risk making a move. I had to stall.

"Why'd he do it, Dudley? Why'd your father murder all these boys?"

Tears were now streaming down his cheeks. "He did it for love, I reckon. All I been able to piece together is that he loved this Joshua," he said, and then the whole story tumbled out. It was as if he'd been waiting to have someone to share it with. "My daddy's a sodomite. He's guilty of one of the worst sins in the Bible, and to make it worse, the men, boys, he chose to lie with were . . . colored. My granddaddy, Malachi, he died 'fore I was born, but daddy always said he was one of them Old Testament Christians, and he was a staunch believer in keepin' the colored in their place, and he definitely wouldn't stand for men lying with men. Anyway, when Granddaddy Malachi found daddy and his . . . friend, Joshua, together, he . . . he beat Joshua to death, and made daddy bury him here in the swamp.

His body shook like a dog just come out of the chilly water of a stream.

"That must've done somethin' to daddy's mind. I mean, what else explains what he done. He buried Joshua over there, under that old tree." He pointed at the tree with the shotgun.

"That doesn't explain the other graves, Dudley," I said gently.

"They came later," he said. "I ain't ever got the whole story, only parts, and some I kinda figured out. But, 'bout two years after . . . it happened, daddy saw this colored boy walkin' down the road, and the boy reminded him of Joshua. He stopped him and they started talkin', and I guess somethin' in his mind just snapped. He strangled that boy and buried him here. One time, when he was kinda lucid, he said it was so's Joshua would have company. I think my daddy's brain ain't right, you know, 'cause after that first one, he started doin' it every year on the anniversary of Joshua's death, then, a couple years 'fore he had his stroke and couldn't get around anymore, he started doin' it ever few months. That's why there's so many of 'em."

"When did you learn of this?"

"I think just before I graduated from high school and went off to college," he said. "I came home early one day from football practice, and I saw him headin' down toward the swamp with this bundle in his arms. I got curious, so I followed him. I plumb got sick when I saw what he was doin', and spewed my lunch all over his shoes when he showed me how many was there. I knew then that my daddy was crazy, and all I wanted to do was get away from him, but the whole time I was away at college, I kept worryin' about him. My mama died when I was ten, and I don't think she ever knew, but I reckon she'd of wanted me to take care of him, so I dropped out of college and came back home."

"He was still killing kids?"

His head bobbed up and down, and the tears were streaming freely now. "Yeah, but he was slowing down. He was getting old. Then, he had the stroke and couldn't get out, so it stopped. Right after the stroke, he started losing his memory. Doctors say it's a form of dementia, and eventually, his brain'll just shut down. Until that happens, I got to take care of him. You understand, don't you?" At the end, his voice had risen slightly. A plea for my . . . what?

"I think I do, Dudley," I said. "But, in your father's condition, there's not much anyone can do *to* him, but maybe they could do something *for* him. You know, make his last days more comfortable."

He seemed to be considering it, but then he shook his head. "No, I can't let 'em take him away. Daddy wants to stay here close to Joshua. If they take him away, it might kill him. I'm sorry, but I'm gonna have to kill you."

He looked like he actually meant it; the sorry part; but that didn't amount to a hill of beans. Whether he was sorry he did it or not, I'd be just as dead.

He raised the twin-barrel shotgun and sighted down the barrels. He was about eighteen feet away, just far enough that the pellets would still be in a tight grouping when they reached me. My hand tightened on the handle of the alligator gig. I wasn't going to go down without a fight.

"Drop the shotgun, Dudley," Beauregard Danton's voice boomed. "Drop it, and get down on your knees with your hands on your head."

I could tell from the way his hands tightened on the shotgun, and the manic look in his eyes, that Jarvis had no intention of complying with Danton's command. The sheriff emerged from behind a tree about forty feet behind Jarvis. He was slightly crouched and had his revolver in a two-handed grip.

"I said, drop the shotgun, Dudley. I don't want to have to shoot you, but I will if you don't put that gun down and do what I told you."

Jarvis, the shotgun still pointing at me, turned his head slowly to the side. He could still watch me out of the corner of his eye, but I wasn't sure he could see Danton clearly. I edged forward another few inches.

"This don't concern you, sheriff," he said. "You ought to go on back to town."

"Can't do that, Dudley; you know that. Now, for the last time, put the shotgun down."

Now, my attention was properly focused. A narrow cone, which primarily included Dudley Jarvis, with Danton on the periphery, had about 75% of my interest, with the rest scanning everything else. I was particularly watching Jarvis's hands and eyes. Either gives indications of what a person's about to do, but you have to keep scanning back and forth between them rapidly to be sure. Usually, eye movement is the first tell, but unless that's followed by some other body movement, it can cause you to react too quickly and be caught off balance. I caught Jarvis's eye movement, a slight flicker downward toward his hands, and then to his right. That was followed quickly by a tightening of his left hand, the one that would initiate the swing of his shotgun around to his right. It wasn't much, just a twitch of the veins visible on the back of the hands, but it was enough to tell me he'd mentally committed to the action.

What followed unfolded in less than three seconds, a couple of heartbeats, but a lot of things can happen in three seconds. His left hand moved first, bringing the shotgun up to hip level and started the rightward swing. Then his shoulder started swinging right, pulling his head around with it, and his eyes were already tracking to the right, ignoring me and seeking out his intended target—Danton. Danton had his revolver up, but seemed frozen in place, his brain probably barely registering Jarvis's movement yet. I tightened my right hand grip on the gig, the tines of which were resting on the hard earth, and brought it up until it was horizontal and level with my right ear. Sliding my left foot forward a few inches for balance, I aimed at Jarvis's right shoulder, just to the right of where the trapezoid muscle sloped downward, and flung the gig at him as hard as I could, at the same time, letting out a 'yee-ah!' as loud as I could. My shout caused Jarvis to hesitate for a fraction of a second in his half-turned position and start to turn his head back toward me, while the shotgun was still swinging toward the right, just as the three razor-sharp nine-inch long steel tines pierced his shoulder. The sharpened metal must have gone in half an inch, not far enough, I thought, to cause a fatal injury, but deep enough to hurt like hell. The pain in his right side caused an involuntary spasm of his trigger finger, and flame shot from one of the shotgun's barrels. There was a loud boom and a puff of white smoke, followed immediately by a piercing scream from Jarvis and a painful cry from Danton. Blood began to make a shiny dark stain on the back of Jarvis's shirt. The shotgun hung limply in his right hand, while he clawed at his back with his left, finally dislodging the gig, which fell to the ground. Three streams of bright red blood spurted from his back. Beyond him, I saw Danton sprawled on the ground, his right side from shoulder to mid-thigh covered with blood. He grasped his right hand with his left. His revolver lay off to his right. I began to sprint in Jarvis's direction.

The gig must have damaged a muscle. Jarvis couldn't lift the shotgun with his right hand. He shifted his left hand, which was grasping his right bicep, and grasped the shotgun. Unable to lift it left-handed, and still moaning painfully, he shot a murderous glare at me as I approached, turned and ran, limping, off the hummock and into the swamp.

I debated chasing him, but Danton's moans of pain drew my attention to him. He lay as I'd first seen him, on his left side, his left hand still clutching his right wrist, which seemed to be bloodier. His eyes were clenched shut, and he moaned through tightly clenched lips. I checked my run, and turned in his direction.

Kneeling next to him, I probed his left side gently to try and determine the extent of his injuries.

"Ow! Damn, that hurts," he said, finally opening his eyes and mouth and looking up at me.

"How badly?" I asked.

"Lucky . . . you distracted that bastard . . . when you did," he got the words out with a struggle. "He shot . . . too soon. Ow! Just the fringe of the shot caught me, mostly my hand and arm . . . some in my side and my . . . leg. It ain't fatal, but it hurts like hell, 'specially when you poke 'round like that."

"Well, glad to see he didn't kill your sense of humor, sheriff."

"Hmph, take more'n a little double-ought to do that. You gon' sit there and swap war stories, or you gon' help me get out of here?"

"Oh, sorry," I said. "Can you walk?"

He raised his head and nodded. "I'll need a little help, but I can make it."

I grabbed his left arm and helped him rise to a standing position. Putting his left arm around my shoulder, and pacing to avoid taxing his injured leg too much, we headed out of the swamp, in the direction of Winston's house. On the way, I began talking to him, as much to distract him from his injuries as anything else. "I found a graveyard in there, sheriff," I said. "*It's why Dudley Jarvis was so concerned about Winston selling the land."

"I know," he said. "Sound carries farther than most people know in these swamps. I heard him tellin' you 'bout his daddy, just before I drew down on him. Damned if I thought he'd take a shot at me."

"Maybe crazy runs in the family. His old man's got to be bat shit crazy; killing that many kids over the years."

"Yeah, that's for sure, and I think in Dudley's case, the nut didn't fall too far from the tree."

It was reassuring to hear him making a joke of the whole thing. He was clearly in a lot of pain, but he gritted his teeth, hung onto my arm, and kept walking.

We broke out of the cover of the trees before he could answer that, and saw Winston and two sheriff's deputies, one a skinny redheaded white and the other a slightly older muscular black, running in our direction. When our two groups met, the two deputies started for the sheriff, but Winston restrained them with an arm as big as some young tree trunks.

"I got him," he said. He gently took Danton in his massive arms, carrying him as if he was an infant. "One of y'all gon' back to the house and call for an ambulance."

The redhead started to sprint toward the house, but Danton's voice, in a commanding tone despite his injuries, stopped him in his tracks, "Hold it, Roy," he said. "I want you and Devlin to do something else. I can call the ambulance myself. I want y'all to go over to the Jarvis place and arrest Dudley Jarvis for attempted murder, and his old man, Henry, for murder."

"Who'd old man Jarvis murder, sheriff?" the black deputy, Devlin, asked.

"I'd have to look in the old files to tell you their names," Danton said. "That don't matter now, just pick the two of 'em up. I'll call for backup and another ambulance. The old man's a cripple, so you'll need it to take him in."

The two deputies looked confused, torn between their duty as sworn officers of the law to uphold the law, their duty to their boss the sheriff to carry out his orders, and their concern for an injured colleague.

"I know where he's likely to come out of the swamp," I said. "He's injured and won't be moving too fast, so we might actually beat him to the house, and I can explain what happened on the way."

Devlin held up a big dark hand, his pink palm facing me. "It's not such a good idea having a civilian along on an arrest," he said.

"It could get dangerous. Besides, we're going in our car."

"Naw, Devlin," Danton said. "Let him go along. It was Al here that saved my life, and with a gator gig if you can believe it. He ain't no ordinary civilian." Both deputies looked curiously at him. "I'll explain it to you later, just get on over there and arrest that bastard 'fore he skips the county."

They still looked skeptical, but discipline won out. That, and the fact that I'd already started jogging toward the house. The waders, now sticking to my sweaty body, slowed me down, though, and they quickly caught up.

"Slow down there," Roy the redhead said. "You're gonna get heat stroke you keep pushing so hard."

He had a point. I slowed to a walk, a fast walk to their car, stopping at the house only long enough to shuck the waders and put on my black boots. By the time their cruiser, which Roy had driven like he was trying out for a NASCAR race, was within sight of the Jarvis farmhouse I'd filled them in on what I'd found in the swamp and what Jarvis had told me. Roy fishtailed to a stop in the front yard, throwing up a ten-foot-high cloud of reddish dust. They got out and both both drew their 9mm sidearms as we approached the building.

"You say he had a shotgun?" Devlin asked me.

"Yeah, but I stuck the gig in his right shoulder. I don't think he'll be able to shoot with that hand."

"Hell, off-hand shooting with a shotgun's just about as dangerous anyway," he said. "You stay behind us, just in case."

I'd been wrong about Jarvis's injuries making it possible for us to beat him home. Caution, however, proved unnecessary.

Chapter 30

When Devlin, the bigger of the two, kicked in the front door of the Jarvis house after shouting, 'Sheriff's office, open up,' twice, and entered in a crouch with his handgun in a two-hand shooting stance, with Roy to his left, doing the same, and me following behind, we found a macabre, bloody, surreal scene like something out of a Sam Peckinpah movie.

Henry Jarvis, a shrunken shell of a man, with wisps of stringy white hair like uncolored cotton candy sticking out from his narrow head in all directions, an unfocused look in his watery blue eyes, and a tattered patchwork quilt across his bony knees, sat in a wheelchair, his cadaverous head moving from side to side, a rivulet of spit leaking out from between his cracked lips, and his body shaking. He didn't even seem aware of our presence. Nor did he seem aware of the body on the floor in front of the wheelchair, even though the right wheel had become entangled with the outthrust left hand.

Dudley Jarvis lay face down, his left hand reaching toward the wheelchair, and now caught in the spokes, bending them and pulling them apart. His right arm was at his side, and like the back of his shirt was black with blood. The shotgun he'd been carrying lay a little behind him on the floor. It was shiny with smeared blood. A thick pool of blood, turning black and congealing, flowed out from him on both sides, making a kind of butterfly pattern on the planks of the wood floor. His eyes were open and staring as his father's. I didn't need a doctor to tell me he was dead. When he wrenched the gig from his back, in addition to damaging muscle, he must have nicked a blood vessel, and just managed to make it back to the house before bleeding out.

"Shit," Roy said, putting his hand over his mouth and nose.

"Yeah," Devlin said, forcing a look of calm, but his brown face was looking a little ashy. "He must've shit himself when he died."

Like cops, firemen, and EMTs everywhere, using gallows humor to mitigate the effect of some of the shit they see—no pun intended. The smell, though, was enough to make you want to puke your guts out; a combination of voided bladder and bowels, and the sickly, metallic smell of blood combine to produce a vomit-inducing sensation topped only by the smell of rotting flesh.

The elder Jarvis seemed immune to the odor and oblivious to the sight. He just sat there for the longest time, drooling and staring at nothing. Then, the strangest thing happened. If I hadn't been looking at him at the time, I wouldn't have believed it.

His eyes changed. The vacant look vanished, and was replaced by a cold, calculating look of cunning that sent ice daggers racing down my spine and caused my sphincter to clutch up tight. And, that evil old son of a bitch was looking directly at me.

"Joshua, it's you," he said in a cracked, nasal voice that seemed to echo off the walls. "You come back." He raised his bony arm and when the sleeve of his robe fell back I could see the bones through his paper-thin flesh, and pointed a gnarled, bony finger at me.

"What the fuck's he talking about?" Roy asked.

I gulped. I'm seldom freaked, but this had me seriously freaked out. "Joshua was a childhood friend of his," I said in a shaky voice. "His father killed him and made Henry here bury him in the swamp."

"Shit," Roy said again.

"Double shit," Devlin added.

They both looked like they were about to get sick.

"Way I figure it," I said. "Is that sometime after that is when he started killing kids that looked like this Joshua, and kept doing it until he had his stroke and couldn't get around."

"Damn, how many you reckon he killed?" The only color left in Roy's young face was the smattering of freckles on his nose.

"Well, I counted a total of sixty-one graves, but I think the one under the tree is this Joshua. *His* father killed him."

"Fuck me! This old bastard killed sixty people," Devlin said. "Hell, he don't look big enough to take down a girl scout."

"You have to remember, these were just kids, and he was nearly an adult when he started," I said. "And, he was a white man. Back in those days when he first started, that alone would've given him an advantage."

"Ho-o-o-ly shit!" Roy shook his head. "A fucking serial killer right here in Coquilla County. That's in-fucking-credible."

"The TV and newspapers gonna have a field day with this one," Devlin said. "Gonna get Bo reelected for sure."

Small town politics. I chuckled. The weirdness of the scene was beginning to wear off, and they were looking at the possibilities. Of course, they were right. The media would be in a feeding frenzy. Serial killers always make good news. And, a serial killer who had operated for so long right under the noses of the authorities was sure to lead the evening news. It didn't exactly make Danton look good, but considering that Jarvis had killed kids in more than one county, I felt sure he'd find a way to finesse it.

After his initial burst of maniacal sanity, Henry Jarvis had dropped back into whatever mental hidey-hole he inhabited. The satanic glint was gone from his eyes and the vacant stare was back.

I had an overwhelming urge to get the hell as far away from this place as possible.

"Hey, guys," I said. "Shouldn't you be calling the meat wagon for the stiff and an ambulance for the old guy?"

"Uh, yeah sure," Devlin said. "And, I guess we're gonna need to throw up some crime scene tape around the house."

"Don't forget to save some for the swamp," I said.

Chapter 31

At 10:00 the next morning, Winston, Rowena and I were sitting in a brightly-lit hospital room at Coquilla Sanitarium in Jacksonville, the main hospital for the county. Beauregard Danton, as befitting his position as county sheriff, was in a private room with a deputy guarding the door. The young towheaded cop, who looked barely old enough to shave, recognized Winston and Rowena, but gave me a squinty-eyed look until Winston introduced me as his cousin. Danton had his bed cranked to a sitting position, and sat with his back propped up by pillows, a meal tray across his lap. His right side, most of his arm, his ribs and the top of his right thigh were swathed in white bandages, and he was frowning down at the little plastic cup of red Jell-O, and the plastic plate with limp string beans, a lump of what looked like library paste, and a greasy gray square.

"Can you believe the swill they feed you in this place? I gotta git out of here so I can get me some real food," he said. He was pouting like a little kid.

Winston had carried a plastic bag, which he concealed under his light jacket when we'd entered the ward. He now pulled it out.

"I kinda figured you'd be sick of hospital grub," he said. "So, I brung you some of Rowena's fried chicken and some biscuits with honey."

Danton smiled, and his eyes glistened.

"Winston, Winston," he said. "That's why you're my best friend. You always take good care of me."

"I figure you'd do the same for me." Winston looked around furtively before handing the bag over.

Danton opened the bag and stuck his face into the opening, taking a couple of deep breaths. When he pulled his face out, he had the look of a kid who has just spotted a new BB gun under the tree at Christmas.

"Oh man, that smells so good," he said. "Rowena, you are without a doubt, the best cook this side of the Mississippi."

Rowena smiled. "Well, stop trying to butter me up, and dig in before it gets too cold."

"Or before the ward nurse comes in and takes it from you," Winston said.

He thrust his hand in and withdrew a drumstick. The aroma immediately began to fill the room as he began ripping the crispy, golden brown meat from the bone. In seconds, he was holding a bone that had been picked clean; even the tiny pieces of gristle were gone. He followed the drumstick with one of the hockey-puck sized biscuits, making ooh and aah sounds as he chewed.

He'd just pulled out a second piece of chicken, a wing, and begun gnawing on it, when a slightly overweight nurse, her blonde hair pulled back into a bun, and her wrinkled, faded green scrubs straining to contain her huge breasts, walked into the room. The name tag on her left breast identified her as RN Wickersham, D.

"Is that fried chicken I smell, Sheriff Danton?" Her voice was stern, but I saw a twinkle in her green eyes.

"Urmph," Danton said around a mouthful of chicken.

"What was that?" She faced him, her hands on ample hips. "What'd you say?"

He swallowed and looked up at her with a hang dog expression. "Aw, come on, Doris," he said. "You know this hospital food ain't fit for human consumption. I have to have something I can recognize, not this gray and plastic stuff."

"I'm 'fraid that's my fault," Winston said before she could respond. "Fried chicken's his favorite, and I kinda figured it'd help him get better."

The blonde smiled at Danton and winked at Winston. "You're probably right 'bout the food. Never ate any of it myself. Okay, I won't report you, just don't leave a mess. I was coming to check your vitals, but I can give you time to digest your meal. I'll be back in ninety minutes, and I don't want to see any sign of non-hospital food, you got that?"

"Urmph." Danton swallowed. "Yes'm, there won't be no sign, I promise."

She was chuckling as she left the room.

"How are you doing, sheriff?" I asked.

He stopped chewing long enough to smile at me. "Hey, Al, call me Beauregard, or better yet, Bo, that's B-O, and don't you say shit about deodorant, Winston." He pointed a finger at my cousin. "Anyway, thanks to you, I'm alive, and actually not in such bad shape. They plucked a hundred and sixteen pellets out of my hide, mostly in the fleshy parts of my arm and elbow and a few in my hip, side and thigh. Couple of 'em nicked my fingers, so I ain't gon' be pluckin' a guitar for a while."

"You don' know how to play no guitar, Bo," Winston said.

"Okay, so I won't be learnin' to play the guitar for a while." He snorted. "But, I'll be out of here in a couple days and back to work." He looked seriously at me. "I mean it, Al, you saved my life. If you hadn't distracted that bastard, he'd of had me cold and I would've caught the full load of that buckshot right in the gut." He shuddered.

"Hey, it was nothing." It wasn't actually *nothing.* I mean, I'd used a damn alligator gig, an oversized fork, against a madman with a double barreled shotgun, and come out of it alive—*and* saved the life of the local sheriff to boot. That was actually pretty big. If I'd done something like that back in DC, the papers, especially my favorite reporter, Lucy Mendez, a features writer for the *Washington Post,* would have been all over it. Coquilla County didn't have a daily, and the *Houston Chronicle* and *Dallas Morning News* hadn't picked it up yet. They'd be descending upon the county like a plague of locusts once word got out, but I'd be—hopefully—long gone by then. I'd let Danton, Bo, have the glory on this one. "I'm just happy you're okay."

"You and me both. Say, Devlin and Roy dropped in this mornin' early," he said. "They were up all night with the state police and some forensics technicians up from Houston, combing that swamp. They found a total of seventy-two graves, some of 'em they think go back to the 1950s, and all of 'em young colored, African-American men between the ages of thirteen and sixteen." He stopped talking and took a deep breath. "It's gon' take 'em months to ID them poor kids, if they ever can."

Rowena wiped away a tear. "I feel so sorry for their families, not knowing all this time."

"Well, maybe now we can give 'em some peace and closure," Danton said. "At least, as many as I can."

"What's gonna happen to the old man?"

"Ain't nobody home in that head of his." He shook his head. "And, he probably ain't got long to live anyway. They'll lock him away in a padded room in the state asylum until he dies."

"Then, I suppose he'll be buried in the prison graveyard?"

"Naw, they'll pro'bly ship him back here and let us bury him in the family plot over to the church between his wife and son."

"Hardly seems fair considering what he did," I said. "If there's an afterlife, it's good to know he'll be disappointed that he wasn't laid to rest next to his friend Joshua."

"There is that." Danton chuckled. "I guess there's some justice in the world after all."

"What I don't understand," I said. "Is how he could kill so many over such a long period of time and no one ever knew."

Danton's expression clouded, and he stared at the wall opposite the foot of his bed.

"It wasn't 'till about six or eight years ago that anybody paid any attention to it," he said. "Some goy from one of the state universities was doing research on missing kids, and he run across it. We had a few over the years here in Coquilla County, but there was others from surrounding counties, and nobody'd ever tied 'em together 'till this fella did.

He looked immensely weary . . . and sad.

"Last one was 'round ten, eleven years ago, that was after I'd been sheriff a while. Missing kid was thirteen, from a sharecropper family up in north county. His poppa done sent him into town to buy some seed and he never come back. We searched high and low for more'n two weeks, but never found a trace. Ever body said he pro'bly just run away. Makes sense sort of . . . life as a sharecropper ain't easy, and I imagine a young man wants somethin' better for himself. Anyways, it wasn't 'till this researcher come 'round askin' questions that we saw the pattern. 'Course, the cases were so widespread, there was no way to establish a pattern, and none of 'em was ever within ten miles of the Jarvis place."

"The old man was certifiable," I said. "But, he was pretty smart. He might never have been found out if it hadn't been for Caldwell's attempted land scam."

He chuckled. "Yeah. What is it they say, 'bout clouds and silver linings. Speakin' of which, Winston, I hear he made you a new offer."

"Shoot, Bo, you know he did." My cousin beamed down at him. "He say he pretty sure they's a lot of natural gas under my property, and I'm liable to make a couple million dollars over the next four or five years."

"Whew!" Danton whistled. "That's a damn sight more'n a hundred thousand, now ain't it?"

"What's gonna happen to Caldwell?" I asked.

"Hell if I know," Danton said. "And, frankly, I don't give a rat's ass. I pure dee would've loved to be able to lock his ass up, but there wasn't enough of a case. Global Energy's gon' have a problem, though, 'cause a reporter from the *Houston Chronicle* done got wind of the story, and they's running a big piece on it."

"I guess the rats will be scrambling," I said. "Well, look, sheriff, I just wanted to make sure you were okay."

"You leavin'?" He looked at Winston.

"Yeah, I gotta get back home."

"Well now, I hope you think fo this as your home. You come back down and me and Winston can take you fishin'."

He held out his un-bandaged left hand. I clasped it.

"I'll keep that in mind," I said.

I wouldn't. I'd no intention of ever coming back to Coquilla County. The look on Winston's face told me that he knew that as well.

Charles Ray

Chapter 32

A t 4:30 pm the next day, I was strolling out of the arrivals building at Dulles International Airport in Herndon, Virginia, just south of the District. I'd lucked out and snagged a seat on a nonstop United Airlines flight from Houston that arrived at Dulles at a little after 4:00. The three-hour flight, crammed into an aisle seat in economy class was bearable—just—but, it beat having to do a layover of anything from an hour in Atlanta to over six hours in Raleigh, North Carolina, or even worse in my view, flying past DC to Chicago, and then flying back. Whoever does airline flight routes must take acid before sitting down to figure them out, or else they're non-flyers themselves. Airline routes make about as much sense as their fares and fees, in other word, they make no sense.

I'd driven to Houston the night before and stayed at one of the airport hotels in order to make my early morning flight, and on the TV in my room I learned that I'd also been successful in settling my cousin's land situation. Midway through the evening news, a spokesman for Global Energy Corporation was filmed explaining that the company had concluded several lucrative mineral leasing contracts in the small town of Poseyville, giving them access to new natural gas deposits that would help turn the ailing company's fortunes around. Almost as an afterthought, the spokesman, an elfin looking man with a hairline well north of the top of his egg-shaped head, said that two Global executives had been dismissed from the company for engaging in activities 'not in keeping with Global's ethical standards.' Alan Grayson, chief of security, and Loren Caldwell, VP for acquisitions, the spokesman said, had misrepresented the company in their dealings with landowners, and the company had, therefore, no alternative but to 'sever all ties with them.' As I watched the little elf talk, I could see the signs that he was reading a well-rehearsed script, and was lying through his expensively-capped teeth. But, hey, Winston and the other farmers got a good deal out of it. Global would drill for natural gas on Winston's land, and in return would pay him rent and a percentage of whatever they found, which, if what they said was accurate, came out to a hell of a lot more than one hundred thousand dollars. And, when the gas was tapped out, or depleted, or whatever they call it in the energy industry, they would restore it to its original condition and leave. A win-win for everyone, so I had to wonder why they would have tried the scam of outright purchase in the first place. Of course, I really knew the answer. Greed, pure and simple. Why take 75 percent of the pie when you can get 90 or 100? Money might not be the root of *all* evil—Henry Jarvis and his warped son were proof of that—but, it sure caused people to do some pretty mean things.

All in all, as I strolled through the glass doors and onto the lower sidewalk just down from the taxi area, I felt good about myself. I'd ensured fairness for a bunch of farmers, one of whom was kin, and I'd brought a vicious serial killer to justice—sort of.

When I looked to the left and saw my green VW Bug make the turn at the end of the concrete rail and come my way, I felt even better. Even at a great distance, I could see the glint of the sun off Sandra's golden hair.

I'd called her from Houston just before takeoff and given her my arrival time. She'd timed it well, arriving must minutes after me and my luggage stepped onto the sidewalk in front of the arrivals hall. There were only a few people waiting for rides near me, but a long line coming out of the door for the 'Washington Flyer Taxi' service.

The sun was still pretty high, and the air was warm and humid, but it felt like a balmy autumn day compared to the sticky heat in Houston.

As the Bug, my nickname for my car, drew closer, I waved. Sandra's left arm emerged through the window and she waved back.

I was stepping off the curb when she pulled over a bit and stopped. I opened the door, tossed my baggage into the back seat, and eased my frame into the passenger seat. She leaned over and our lips met. She smelled great and tasted even greater. After such a deep, satisfied kiss, I wanted to pull her into my arms, but the seatbelt across her ample bosom made that impossible, so I satisfied myself with nuzzling her neck.

"I missed you, babe," she said.

It had been just about a week, but it felt longer than that.

"Missed you, too," I said.

"You want to drive?"

"Nah, I'm good." I pulled my seatbelt across my chest and snapped it shut. "Let's go home."

She pulled away from the curb and drove smoothly past the main terminal, around past the private aviation terminal, and into the loop that exits onto the Dulles Airport access road. Traffic exiting the airport was picking up, but spread out once it hit the access road, so pretty soon, we were sipping along at sixty miles per, heading east toward the I-495 Beltway and home.

Once she'd settled in the right lane, she turned her head partway and looked at me. I'd just been sitting there, drinking in her beauty.

"How was your trip?" she asked.

"Oh, not too bad I suppose. You know what they say about Texas, the best view is it receding in your rearview mirror."

It was an old, lame joke, but I never tired of it. She laughed. Because she loved me not because it was funny.

"Did you get your cousin's problem solved?"

"Yep."

"Just yep?

"He was being scammed by this energy company. Oh, they claim it was this rogue exec operating on his own, but I know better. Anyway, they signed a pretty good leasing agreement with Cousin Winston, and he'll soon be a wealthy man."

We drove on a little further in silence except for the rush of passing traffic and the whining of the VW's tires on the highway.

"Anything else interesting happen?"

"Why do you ask?"

"I know that pensive look, the one you get when something bad has happened."

That's the problem. She knows me all too well. It's damn hard to keep anything from her, and even though all I wanted to do was forgot, I found myself telling her about the graves in the swamp, and Dudley Jarvis bleeding out at his invalid father's feet. When I finished, I sat there, gazing out the front window, watching the pavement slide under us. She gripped the wheel hard, her knuckles white, and stared straight ahead as well.

Finally, she glanced over at me.

"It must have been terrible for you."

"I've had better days."

"At least, the families of some of those boys will have closure."

"Yeah, there's that."

"I'm not sure I believe in the hereafter, but if there is one, their spirits can now be at peace."

Damn, that's what Sara's voice said in my dream. I suppose she was right. If such things as spirits exist exposing what had happened to them should bring them peace. I wasn't so sure about myself, though. I'd slept well in the airport hotel. But, when I woke up that morning, my first thought was the sight of all those graves, and those pitifully small skeletons.

"Yeah," I said. "Now, they can be at peace."

"I'm so glad you're home," she said.

I looked from her, the expression on her face placid, and her blue eyes watching the traffic ahead and in the rear view mirror, to the countryside zipping by on either side of the car, the shopping center decks visible from below, the high-rise office buildings and condos, and the green space—lots and lots of green space. It looked peaceful and idyllic. Of course, underneath, it's anything but. The Washington area is a chaotic place, with as much diversity, intrigue and mayhem as you'll find in any of the world's major cities. But, it still manages to cling to a kind of big town persona. The traffic is unbelievably, and the politicians and lobbyists constantly poison the atmosphere with their shenanigans. Why on earth would anyone want to live in this place?

Hell, I don't know. I just know that at that moment, I wouldn't have wanted to be anyplace else. I laid my left hand lightly on her right hand, not enough pressure to affect her ability to steer the car, but enough that we could share each other's body heat.

"I'm glad to be home," I said.

Books by this author:

Al Pennyback mysteries
Color Me Dead
Memorial to the Dead
Deadline
Dead, White, and Blue
A Good Day to Die
The Day the Music Died
Die, Sinner
Deadly Intentions
Death by Design
Till Death Do Us Part
Deadly Dose
Dead Man's Cove
Dead Men Don't Answer
Deadly Paradise
Kiss of Death
Death in White Satin
Death and Taxis
Deadbeat
A Deadly Wind Blows
Death Wish
Deadly Vendetta
A Time to Kill, A Time to Die
Dead Ringer
Death of Innocence
Dead Reckoning
Murder on the Menu
Over My Dead Body

The Buffalo Soldier series:

Buffalo Soldier: Trial by Fire
Buffalo Soldier: Homecoming
Buffalo Soldier: Incident at Cactus Junction
Buffalo Soldier: Peacekeepers
Buffalo Soldier: Renegade
Buffalo Soldier: Escort Duty
Buffalo Soldier: Battle at Dead Man's Gulch
Buffalo Soldier: Yosemite
Buffalo Soldier: Comanchero
Buffalo Soldier: Range War
Buffalo Soldier: Mob Justice
Buffalo Soldier: Chasing Ghosts
Buffalo Soldier: The Piano
Buffalo Soldier: Family Feud

Ed Lazenby mysteries

Butterfly Effect
Coriolis Effect
The Cat in the Hatbox

Other fiction

Angel on His Shoulder
She's No Angel
Child of the Flame
Pip's Revenge
Wallace in Underland
Further Adventures of Wallace in Underland
Dead Letter and Other Tales
The White Dragons

The Dragon's Lair
Dragon Slayer
The Last Gunfighters
The Culling
Frontier Justice: Bass Reeves, Deputy
    U.S. Marshal
Angel on His Shoulder-Revised Edition
Battle at the Galactic Junkyard
Mountain Man
Devil's Lake

Nonfiction
Things I Learned from My Grandmother About
    Leadership and Life
Taking Charge: Effective Leadership for the
    Twenty-first Century
Grab the Brass ring
African Places: A Photographic Journey
    Through Zimbabwe and southern Africa
A Portrait of Africa
There's Always a Plan B
In the Line of Fire: American Diplomats in
    the Trenches
Advice for the Insecure Writer
Looking at Life Through My Lens

Children's books

The Yak and the Yeti
Samantha and the Bully
Molly Learns to Share
Where is Teddy?
Catie and Mister Hop-Hop
Tommy Learns to Count
Catie Goes to School

About the Author

Charles Ray has been writing fiction since his teens. He won a Sunday school magazine writing contest when he was thirteen, and having his byline on a short story published in a national publication forever hooked him on writing. During his time in the army (1962-1982) he often moonlighted as a newspaper or magazine journalist, and was the editorial cartoonist for the Spring Lake (NC) News, a weekly newspaper, during the 1970s. In addition to his writing, he was an artist/cartoonist and photographer for a number of publications, including Ebony, Eagle and Swan, and Essence, and had a monthly cartoon feature and did several covers for Buffalo, a now-defunct magazine that was dedicated to showcasing the contributions of African-Americans to the country's military history.

After retiring from the army, he joined the U.S. Foreign Service, and served as a diplomat in posts in Asia and Africa until his retirement in 2012. He has worked and traveled throughout the world (Antarctica is the only continent he hasn't visited), and now, as a full time writer, continues to globetrot looking for interesting things to write about, draw, or take pictures of.

A native of Texas, he now calls Maryland home. For more on his writing and other projects, check one of the following Web sites:

http://charlesaray.blogspot.com
http://charlieray45.wordpress.com
http://www.twitter.com/charlieray45
http://www.facebook.com/charlieray45
http://www.flickr.com/photos/charlesray45/
http://www.viewbug.com/member/charlesray

Author's photograph by Denise Ray-Wickersham

www.ingramcontent.com/pod-product-compliance
Lightning Source LLC
Chambersburg PA
CBHW061943170626
46813CB00006B/2511